Penguin Books
NIGHT

KT-131-416

Edna O'Brien was born in the West of Ireland and now lives in London. One of Britain's most popular and respected contemporary writers, she is author of *The Country Girls*, *Girl with Green Eyes* (first published as *The Lonely Girl*), *Girls in their Married Bliss*, *August is a Wicked Month*, *Casualties of Peace*, *The Love Object* (short stories), *A Pagan Place*, *Zee and Co.*, *Mother Ireland*, *A Scandalous Woman and Other Stories*, *Johnny I hardly knew you*, *Arabian Knights* (photography by Gerard Klijn), *Mrs Reinhardt and Other Stories*, *Returning* and *A Christmas Treat*. Edna O'Brien was awarded the *Yorkshire Post* Novel Award in 1971. *The Collected Edna O'Brien*, containing nine novels, was published in 1978, and *Some Irish Loving*, an anthology of prose and poetry, in 1979. Her most recent publication is *A Fanatic Heart*, a selection of stories.

Edna O'Brien

Night

Penguin Books

Penguin Books Ltd, Harmondsworth, Middlesex, England
Viking Penguin Inc., 40 West 23rd Street, New York, New York 10010, U.S.A.
Penguin Books Australia Ltd, Ringwood, Victoria, Australia
Penguin Books Canada Limited, 2801 John Street, Markham, Ontario, Canada L3R 1B4
Penguin Books (N.Z.) Ltd, 182–190 Wairau Road, Auckland 10, New Zealand

First published by Weidenfeld & Nicholson 1972
Published in Penguin Books 1974
Reprinted 1976, 1977, 1978, 1980, 1984, 1985, 1987

Made and printed in Great Britain by
Richard Clay Ltd, Bungay, Suffolk
Set in Linotype Baskerville

For the Lads

She is far from the land
Where her young hero sleeps

(Song)

The original Hooligans were a spirited Irish
family whose proceedings enlivened the drab
monotony of life in Southwark towards the end
of the nineteenth century.

E. Weekley

One fine day in the middle of the night, two dead men got up to fight, two blind men looking on, two cripples running for a priest and two dummies shouting Hurry on. That's how it is. Topsy-turvy. Lit with blood, cloth wick and old membrane. Milestones, tombstones, whetstones and mirrors. Mirrors are not for seeing by, mirrors are for wondering at, and wondering into. There was a piece of glass by which we tried to catch and contain the sun's fire. It must have been called a sunglass. There is so little and so fucking much. Half a lifetime. Felt, seen, heard, not fully felt, most meagrely seen, scarcely heard at all, and still in me, rattling, like a receding footfall, or Count Dracula's swagger.

I am in a bed, a fourposter no less, satinized headboard, casters. Paws come out from underneath the well of the bed, all vying for a handshake, some gloved, some ungloved. The more I wrestle with sleep the more it ducks me, I am beckoning to it, beseeching. There are moments when it seems imminent, but then it vanishes, like a cloud formation or someone on rollerskates. I've had better times of course – the halcyon days, rings, ringlets, ashes of roses, shit, chantilly, high teas, drop scones, serge suits, binding attachments, all that. I used to have such a penchant for feelings, now, I feel as much for the woman in the train who had the flushes, as for the woman Lil who bore me.

Outside it is blustery. In the occasional lull I think I hear an owl. Of course I always hear the cars, their drone in the distance, cars going too fast at night. There could be an owl since we are on the outskirts of a city and there are trees to roost in. They too are creaking and groaning. I am counting sheep but they are tumbling into one another and I see nothing but rumps of greying fleece, ruddled at that, and as for the ploy of counting apples, it is too playful, too strenuous. Still, one has to pass the time, the leisure hours, the resting hours, knit up the ravelled sleeve of care. Jesus. Buckets of time, you put your hand into it, deep down as far as the elbow, and it is like putting your hand into the abyss. So slowly does time pass, that is if it passes at all. Still, the Christmases rip around quick enough, the giving and taking, the Yule-tide grog, the guzzle beneath the parasitic mistletoe. Only the minutes are rugged.

I knew a man once that saw time as loaves of bread, feasted on it, gorged, got overbloated, lost his desire, became a toper instead. I knew another that squashed eggs in his hand, existed for that sound, that crunching sound when he squelched them in his fist, made snowballs of them and threw them shell and all at whoever he happened to sight. A cretin. I've met them all, the cretins, the pilgrims, the scholars and the scaly-eyed bards prating and intoning for their bit of cunt. More of them anon.

I have the curtains drawn, the old clausilium shut, tight, so it ought to be safe enough, it ought. I take a tablet, break it down its central line and swallow one half, with some of the waters of the Malvern hills. I've always had a taste for spring waters, sparkling waters and sturgeons' eggs. I lie with my God, I lie without my God. Into the folds of sleep. Oh Connemara, oh sweet mauve hills, where will I go, where will I not go, now?

Fucking nowhere.

I say seven and think it means something. The figure slides across the page or the blackboard or the sweet sky or the sawdust floor and though it tells me something, like the cost of the joyride, or what filly to back, or how long more the journey, the immediate journey that is, it does not tell me what I need to know. Not that I know what I need to know. Not that I do. I am a woman, at least I am led to believe so. I bleed et cetera. And those noises, and those sighs, and those murmurs, and those innuendoes, and those emanations, and those come-hithers, and those coo-coos, issue from me faithfully like buntings. Not to mention the more bucolic sounds, the ones in sly reserve, the choice slushings of the womb which have ogled many another by means of gurgle, nuance, melody, ditty and crass babbling supplication. A dab hand at it I was. As aforesaid I have met bards and knackers. Along the wayside. They told me many a tale, spun me many a yarn, swindled me as often as not. I bathed their feet, had ointments, mused, groped in the dark, looked up to the constellations, identified the Plough and the Milky Way, said most lachrymose things.

There are so many waysides that one mistakes them sometimes for the real route.

I have had unions, tête-à-têtes, ripping times, gay collisions. All sickeningly predictable like a doh ray me fa. Simply did they start up the perturberations, the springtime spawn, the yea-nay, the boogie-woogie. Result, more blasted birth or more blasted arrested birth. And hark, a population problem. Solution. *Nota bene*. A hard ebony cock secure within the lassies and the myriad others, that is to say the poor male human rejects, displayed upon a clothes-line, white, bloodless, jovial, obedient; twittering, hanging, maybe even fluttering, like sparrows perhaps, or socks, or sloths or clothes-pegs proper. Hosannah.

We had a clothes-line in Coose, in fact we had two. One adjacent to the back kitchen, ideal for small things such as teacloths, dribblers and bibs, then one farther away, on a hill, open to the prevailing winds, that served for sheets, blankets, quilts, eiderdowns, pillowcases, bolster cases and the Boss's lugubrious long johns. Quite a formidable place on account of the force of the trade winds, and the clothes that flap-flapped and the sight of Lil frequently rushing out to retrieve things at the first onslaught of the rain and the hails that were wizard both for their frequency and their velocity. A bit like the sea although it was green and had thickets and the different field flowers in the different field months. So lying here I think of there. God blast it. As if there was nothing else, as if there was no one else. One's kith, one's kin – Boss, Lil, Tutsie and the inimitable Dr Flaggler. No forgetfulness within, or without. The heart in its little swoon, in accord, sometimes in discord, and a note of solemn music, a refrain, for ever being struck up within one, saying thy mother, thy father, thy spouse, thy son, thyself. Others too, though never the mob, never enough of mob. I have written some nauseating letters – 'you touched my heart, you touched my cunt, I touched yours' and so on and so forth. Devouring, cloying, calumnious. All of those missives I have kept in reserve because to act as nonsensical as that, without presently dying would be the most clownish of my many clownish actions. I have even made a written request to be buried on an island in the vicinage of Coose, a woeful place surrounded by choppy waters and presided over by a pair of unpropagating swans. An affirmative involves the goodwill of the hierarchy and also of the lady butcher who has leased the grazing rights, *ad infinitum*. Its features consist of tombs, tumuli, vaults, boulders, a round tower, turds, toadstools and bullocks all scratching and munching and chewing their cuds. No doubt, on frosty mornings it is regaling to witness their vapours, the numerous vapours rising up, the flowers congealed in the ice, splendid plumes of grass, the peckled shimmer of the headstones and the thistles lording it like starched cockades. But mere postulation, to want to lie there when I am incapable of living anywhere within its precincts. Is it that I imagine death to be the apotheosis of loneliness, to do away with a lesser loneliness, the force, puniness and shackle of which has kept me captive in towns and cities, where I have forgotten the fact that earth and running water lie somewhere underneath the vast complex of concrete and sewerage and rubble and weed and fag-ends and grating and shit. In yon High Street the tyres play havoc with the shit, especially the double tyring of lorries and pantechnicons. I often say 'Ah, to sink into it at last, to say yea instead of nay to the lambative stink and smear of it all.' Good-bye to daisies and plankton, good-bye to the mavis, the missel and the white-bodied thrush. It is the dunghill ethos, is it not. Another thing that might have influenced my decision about the island is the banishment of it. The truth is I do not wish to lie with my own kith and kin. Another blow for King James and for the green. I do not want to lie with anyone else's kith and kin either. One for King Billy. I have no desire, not even in deathbed slobber, to be lumped in with other people and have them flustering around me and vice versa. Think of the tenderness we would have to purport, the subsequent niceties, the clacking of tongues, handshakes, boneshakes, in order to live, middlingly peaceably, together for a long time, for ever maybe. Maybe. I want to be by myself at last and to be robbed of that stupid, suppurating malady they call hope. Not to be a member of the communion of saints or gods or demi-gods or fathers or mothers or grandfathers or grandmothers or brothers or sisters or brethren of any kind, germaine to me through consanguinity, affinity, or any other kind of linear or genitive or collateral bond. To face the music at last. To be on one's tod. Do I mean it? Apparently not. I am still snooping around, on the lookout for pals, pen pals, pub pals, cronies of any kind, provided they know their place, keep at distance, stay on the leash, leave me my soul's crust, and my winding dirging effluvias.

There was a time when I made jam and met my son Tutsie, as he came through the school gates. A straggler, nearly always the last, always tarrying. Big lad now, has a quarter share in a jeep, and is touring the world. Said he wanted to reach places that others hadn't percolated to. Taciturn, always was. He loved the animals, had a way of taming them. He stayed on a train once, crouched down, just to be near a dachshund, stroking it. When at first he was tonsured and I used to be putting a bonnet on him, the crown of his head spoke to me of former massacres, his little bones used to suggest holocausts. Then sprouts, like toothbrushes came standing on his head, and then it began to grow in ringlets, long flaxen curls. I have these locks, and his milk teeth in a little chain purse, stored for his children. I am eager for them. The purse is in the blanket along with the rest of my belongings. A mother's love, like yeast, multiplying, the spores rising up over the lid of the world, too much. Grandiloquent pees he did in the municipal parks, to keep tow with the fountains. The janitors and keepers used to get us to scarper, crotchety people keepers and those in authority. I am in authority here but it's negligible.

One day a week I bought a lollipop for him. That was a Thursday. The Thursdays have become all one, the Thursdays of his childhood and mine, and perhaps yours? Ring a ring o' rosy, haisha haisha, we all fall down. The dye of the lollipop used to rubify the colour of his lips, dribble down on to his chin, drop on to the nap of his dufflecoat and then very deftly his little tongue came out to retrieve it. He even retrieved it from the coat or retrieved as much of it as hadn't soaked into the pile. Our treat was sherbet. It caught in the throat. The grains lodged in the tastebuds and spread behind the nose and made all the inside of the mouth areas itch with pleasure. I suppose mouths experience it first, the resuscitation, the life thrill. Also there was a little wooden spatula with it, sturdy enough to press the tongue flat, much preferable to Dr Rath's implement for when he got people to say Aaaah. It smelt of summer, that sherbert, at least it seems so now.

I try, I try so hard to recollect – not that recollection is of any use – but to remember the then, their countenances, what they wore, what I saw of myself, mis-saw, when I looked into one of the many long, sad, blotched mirrors that fronted the wardrobe doors in that dark rookery that was our house, our homestead. I remember nothing much except the sherbert, its airiness, crêpe dresses with the creeps on them, and a rubber ball mauled by a dog so that its insides were like a frayed old brain falling about. A ball, a dog, a brain?

There weren't enough forks to go around on the days of the threshing, and some workmen, the apish ones, had to wait, malinger, while others hacked their food assiduously before passing on the ungainly utensils. Ah yes, it is trickling through. Men with caps upon the knee, cloth caps, peaked caps, nosegays in the form of sops of hay, the odd surname such as Dowling or Stack, a bit of a snortle, the numerous pisreogs, the clamorous Banshee, the Buggie man, the geese already ushered to the cornfields to get the leavings, to lunge their black webbed feet into the rails of stubble, to gorge themselves in order to be plump for Christmas. It would have been then autumn. Harvests are. That I do know.

That and the ears of corn, gushes, pouring out of a chute, and the men busy with the pitchforks and the chaff flying, while down in the kitchen cling-clang as the washed forks were put back in the musted drawer. Those showers of corn, in some way connected with a seventh heaven, as was the silver of a chalice and the dunner silver of the one christening mug that the male issue of the family had been presented with, after birth. Silver and gold, gospel and gooseberries, the snagging of same, the benefits of carragheen moss, that cold substance that was liable to wobble when tipped out of its corrugated mould. A trepidation. There were also the hens, moving in and out between the ragwort, the latter gaunt, over-riding the grasses. Cock a doodle doo, monarch of all he surveyed. Afternoons merging into evenings, and such a momentum of tears and for what, and for whom? Evening light, sometimes phosphorescent, in threads, finely spun, melting, molten, like oil, like honey, ladles of light, linking the two worlds, the one where we carried cudgels, the other to which we aspired to go and for which the whole of our living life was a frigging pilgrimage.

Somebody – that tattler Dowling – announced that a tennis court was going to be erected, a hard court of tarmacadam, and that on their weekly half days the shopkeepers, the excise officer and the bank clerks would be able to while away the time in white tuxedos, causing a ball to pass to and fro while some flunkey counted up the winning and the losing scores. Farmers were to be prohibited. When Boss heard that he harangued. He hated to be slighted. His temper rose, causing him to down three of his indigestion tablets which he cracked vehemently with his molars. The precincts smelt of magnesium. Oh Boss, were you ever not on the edge of a cataclasmic ire, with your two brown suits and your white shins that were revealed to all at the ploughing match of Glenstall, the day you got a kick. Incurred a kick from a bay mare and since he was without benefit of leggings or gaimbeaux he was perforce to roll his trousers to look for injuries in case he had to resort to a reprisal such as fisticuffs or calling in the law. 'Buggerotum to tennis,' Boss said, 'a fop's game, clerk's stirabout.' To have known and not known, now that is a glim thing. Glim. Glaucous. To have met and not met, like cyclists, in a spinney at night, cyclists going in opposite directions and passing each other without a greeting, without a snatch of conversation, without a holler; recognizable to each other only by the strength or the weakness of their flashlights, or their tail-lights, or failing such properties, recognized by the sheen of the spokes or the mudguard or the handlebars in the thrall of the night. Not known. So many of our encounters are. Even the gut ones. Especially the gut ones.

The seed of my father I reach out to you, as you once did to me, pitifully, passionately, idiotically, to small avail. What caused us to embark on such a maraud? Her buttocks, flaunched and ordinary, the slit, the slit of absurdity into which we chose to pass. The nearest we ever were. You and I? You or I? Only you, not yet I? Already I, no longer you? A trinity of yobs. In occidental damp and murk. What gave rise to your spasming? A full moon, a half moon, no moon at all, a touch of the madman's wisp, duty, reconciliation, thirst? Anything? The crab delights in soft and unguent places. Bucking maybe and pronouncing fiendish words such as bollocks or jackass or Oirre, upon her. Grunting. I wouldn't put it past you. You shaman you. Already I, with some cursed inkling, some predilection towards shame and calamity and stupor, already liturgicalized before entering that dark, damp, deep seasous place. No choice in the matter.

And still such a long way to go in between stopping and starting and eating Brussels sprouts.

Christmàs is not long gone. It went by without too much event. I did not partake of the sacraments. I received three presents, a nightdress that will be perfect for my lascivious nights, a frothy affair; a casket, and a teacloth which has scripted in it my character according to my astrological sign. If I am well-placed, I am magnanimous, faithful, bashful, aspiring in an honourable way at high matters, a lover of fair dealings, of sweet and affable conversation, wonderfully indulgent, reverencing aged men and fully of charity and godliness. If the stars are ill-placed, then I shall waste my patrimony, suffer everyone to cozen me, am hypocritical and stiffe in maintaining false tenets, am ignorant, careless, gross, of dull capacity and schismatical.

If again I come to love a member of the opposite sex

and even a member of my own sex, I shall try not to gabble. It won't be easy for me, brought up as I was among hens and bullocks and buckets and winds and clothes-lines and people, all gaggling themselves to distraction. But even if I default in that I shall spend my spirit in other things, spirit is spirit the way gut is gut and limestone, limestone.

To see a door close and know that the very last person has gone out, that is a most unsettling thing. No one to call to, no one to cling to, no one. Not even Humpty Dumpty or Old King Cole. I reach out and grip the fur, the grey fur of the ample quilt. Armenian goat as far as I can tell from my desultory knowledge of wild life. A blow. The hairs of this quilt are not nearly sturdy enough to bask in, to tug at, to wallow. They give way. They come off in the fingers as mere tufts. I touch the wall behind the sateen headboard. Knock knock. It is not knife-edged as I feared. Something is. Something goes whirr whirr, like the Duke's lawnmower; and snip snip like blind Dr Rath clipping the stitches. Big ungainly stitches in those days, when Lil gave birth. Black herring-bone stitches made out of catgut, some substance, got from sheep as in the strings of a fiddle. I resemble her, except in one particular. She had a little green floating spot on the white of an eye, a purty little spot it was, and if I am to develop any new characteristics I shall plump for one, one that moves slightly according to the curvature and gaze of the eye. Not a bright green, more or less misted. I think I perceived the bottles of syrup as being shaken while I was still in her, in her chambers. I wrote and asked if she had any inkling, any hunch, about the exact colour of her innards, my earliest known abode. I thought it was very likely she would come up with suggestions, being as she had such a talent for colour schemes in the linoleums, the madeira cakes, the wallpapers, the borderings and the wool rugs that she fashioned through the long nights. I seem to remember streaks of colour, zebras, sometimes pink, sometimes green, sometimes too green, likewise too pink. I reamed off a list, became prodigal, even resorted to shadings. I filched my ideas from nature, various spools of thread, a paint card, seed catalogues and a luxurious sanitary shop where I sometimes go and pretend that I am contemplating buying a topaz bath. I love going there. I dress up in borrowed plumes, look like a toff. I said she might like to be extravagant, she might like to sally into inventiveness, give vent to herself, lie if needs be. No sooner had I posted the letter than I realized what a débâcle I had made. My mother is dead. To make matters worse, my mother is only fairly recently dead and I realized that the postman, who is a dunce and a dunderhead, and bunioned from his peregrinations, would deliver it out of habit. I knew that his feet would conduct him there and some other part of his palsied anatomy would haul the epistle out of his big grey canvas bag, and that he would say, as he so faithfully says, at the sight of any foreign postmark, in sentimental tones, 'Hands across the water.' I realized that Boss would be aghast by the untowardness, by the brazenness, by the cruelty of such an action. Pleasant to know that he could not take action, that he would not be able to throw sticks and stones as they did to Dick Studdard. Water divides us, and more than the nine Dedannan waves at that. Hurray for all waters, spa waters, bog waters, lone wells, tobhairs, lakes, rivers, streams, Baptism fonts and of course the oyster-breeding seas.

Her funeral was a comic event, despite the keenings and the ululations. A sizeable crowd, all in sable, the mourners. Grievously stung they were by nettles that grew in abundance. We took a short cut in order not to have to walk over the bordered paths. It was as if we couldn't get her in quick enough, into the bowels of the earth, where the moles and the sprites are reputed to be, have their intricate routes and conduits. On the way, a bicycle was espied, propped up against a yew tree, a man's bicycle, an upstairs model, flung. Some of the men, the more loquacious ones, interpolated on whose it could be, suggested various names, Christian names and surnames and nicknames, but having reached no conclusion then started to wonder aloud why the owner had left it thus, what importunity had overtaken him, and they agreed that he had either gone because he got taken short, or to have a fit, or to find a well of water, or to pray to God, or to lie down for bucolic reasons with a woman or a travelling woman, or a married woman, or a beast, or no other agent at all. Then came the suggestion that the rider of the bicycle might have been a she who had gone to do any one of the aforementioned things or to deliver herself of a bastard child. Not the most reverential thought. The clay got richer, redder, the deeper they dug. They were quick with the spade, made darty incisions; and of course there were fine manifestations of sorrow – dribbles, sniffles, tears, gulps all stifled by handkerchief or make-do handkerchief. A stripling went by, a fellow with unmatching eyes, looking for sheep of his that had strayed. Five or six. God dammit, a matchless eyed man of miserable means ought to know whether he had lost five sheep or six. Seeing the coffin and the mourners, he realized what he had blundered into and squatting to denote his sympathy, he removed his cap and asked whose funeral it was. At the crucial moment I made an ape of myself, behaved in the following manner. I jumped in, prostrated myself, bawled, and woe betide, a second, a more ludicrous disaster, I sprained my ankle. I need hardly tell you of the furore that ensued. Excitement craned its head. Maybe that is why I jumped in, to leaven the occasion. I doubt it. I lack the talent for instigating comedy. They put it down to grief. Some said a seizure, some said cracked, some said highly strung. Highly strung! I eat like a horse, the reason I eat is to encase my heart in a solid fortress of fat, so that I can at last decently and uneventfully expire without much ado, to return in the end to *materiam primam* whate'er it be.

There were refreshments after the funeral. The catering! She would not have tolerated it. There was spotted dick and big biscuits that were damp, and had somewhere in their lifespan been neighbours to paraffin oil. On the savoury side there were chunks of ham thrown on to plates, some with a dollop of potato salad and others with a yellow piccalilli, depending on the whim of the two serving ladies. The whole event lacked finesse. Naturally there weren't enough chairs. People had to sit on the edges of chairs, which made the cutting of their ham precarious. Then the catsup was thin and scalding and restraint was not executed in the pouring of it. This was due to the seating more than to any avidity. Things were said, not too many things, her praises sung. They discussed her memoriam card, discussed what mottoes it could contain. I had always noticed her penchant for the colloquial, for things like 'The early bird catches the worm,' but I had to sit there and hear the adages of Saints Jerome and Bonaventure trotted out as applicable material. How little we make of what we know of anyone, how little we employ it.

Of course she did not die without a long illness, mothers never do. Fathers likewise.

I went to nurse her, grudgingly, no, not grudgingly, with pangs. Birth pangs, life pangs, death pangs – they must be cousins. She was upstairs, same bed as she had given birth in, had had her lumbago in, and numerous other afflictions. I remained out of the room as much as possible, out in the hallway, humming so that she would know I was there, doing chores. I varnished a floor but the fumes of the turpentine did not agree with her, in other words I varnished half a floor. While in the room I washed her sores, polished the mirrors and made plans

19

for future times – Christmas, holiday and so forth. There is nothing so offensive as hoodwinking the nearly dead. We die by degrees but there is one part of us that decidedly knows when it is all just over. There is one strand of the mind that reckons with that passing over and she was in possession of it. I could hear it, registering, like a clock and invisibly ticking. There was altar wine on the window-sill and it bore a label from the land of Spain. She declined that. It was the priests' wine, the canons'. Poor canons, their old scrotums like dust, shedding maybe, shedding dust. Their organs, pink or whey? Poor canon, he coughed when he came, to shrive her. Not a bit standoffish. No preamble. The sacrament was always under a cloth, a cloth that had little darns in it. She swallowed with agony, to hear her swallow was to have pity for her, the stitches under her throat, jabbing like needles. Some distraction always intervened, like a cat sidled in, a kettle sang, or a bird sang, or something fell off the bed, usually her comb. Once he came with the chalice empty. After that the curate came. Poor canons, old, grey, teetering, lonely and loony, with their frock coats and their faithful housekeepers, that breed of dark warted women that do wait upon them.

I would go out on the landing again and talk in. She saw the treachery of those plans regarding Christmas and holidaying, and her eyes were as daggers, blue, cobalt blue, asking not, not to go. Ranting, raving. I heard things no one ought to hear, no one or everyone. She listened for a lorry going by, mentioned the driver, a big brute she said, bullet-headed, said he could jack it up, referred to his jockstrap, said Off with the jockstrap and fire. When the pain got less or the morphine got more she prayed. How she prayed. How she then smiled. The clouds she said, so similar to the bushes, to the bushiness of the bushes. The clouds had the ramble of bushes. She said why shouldn't she walk and talk, though not even a buzzard was contradicting her. How she grieved. She said you could put all the pleasures that had gone into her life into a little thimble, and she looked for a thimble, though sewing was not one of her accomplishments. The pleasures she listed, a flower between the pages of a book, a journey to America, some hats with veiling, a return journey, and fresh peaches that she put her lips, her teeth, and finally her gums into. She said her little joys ever after were her little pullets, in their dust baths, dozing and sonoring away, cogitating to lay their first egg. She held it somewhere in her mind's hand, the little egg. She scolded a pullet because of laying out, said did they not know there was a henhouse. She went in search of them, calling and cackling and stopped when she came to a mound, and said why shouldn't she risk going up, and in sport crown herself high queen of that place. And again without moving her body except to stir a toe in order to rub another, her head and eyes moved as she went up the mound and she said there was a fine view of the top storey of the house and announced that the slates that had been always missing were still missing. She uttered a snatch of a song, half song, half prayer. She said the place had three trees, a sycamore with its pods flat and empty, an oak and a little hazel bush. She said the bark on the oak was grey and shredding like she was. Then some children went by, a butcher's son, a veterinary surgeon's son, a druggist's son, children all connected with the dark themes of life. Gabbling they were. She searched in the grass pretending to be searching for eggs. It seems they told her to beware of snakes and she said Insolent buggers they were, with their guns and their cowboy caps, and she sent them packing on their way, said No trespassing, no trespassers. And she stayed there and said how she longed for it not to be dark, but to be bright, bright days and shafts of light passing through her and her children all young again and around her as in a needlework, in their frills, in their finery, in their little buttoned boots; and she longed and she longed for it and she reproached God and man and said it was not happening but that everything was getting dark and the mound with it and that the house was waiting for herself to come in and trim the doddery aladdin and light it up. Suddenly she sat up and said was there an R in the month because if so, we were running a risk of pneumonia, sitting out there on damp dunged grass. I said no, which was all I could say. Her eyes were daggers asking not to go, not, not to go. She ran her fingers through the fringes of the coverlet as if they were rings, trinkets, and she said foul words that she could not have known. I had washed the sheets, four sheets washed per day because of the amount she haemorrhaged. We could hear them on the clothes-line, as they flapped about. That, and the noise of the rain, rain of such urgency, blue in the far-off places, colourless close at hand, brown where it lodged, big drops falling on the blades of grass, appointing itself on hedge and grass blade, then more and more, buckets of rain and a wind, a whining wind, and everything shifting, even daisies and dandelions, particularly daisies and dandelions, small things uprooted, and the dogs at the steps moaning to get in to her, dogs wet and sated, sated from killing rabbits, coated in rain but tasting of blood. The dogs, she said. The dogs, I said. She was off on another transport.

Dogs. Some dogs have nice hair, some dogs hunt foxes, cross dogs bite, mountain dogs have stiff coats, dogs drink water and milk, dogs kill cats, dogs eat anything.

A scuttle she said her mind was, clumps where thoughts should be. Big bulbous clumps, black in the interior. She admitted that she was losing her faith. It was forsaking her at the very moment when she needed to have it in order to present her credentials. She raved but then became very coherent in the moments before dying. She said something about a hatpin. It was then I should have quiffed her hair, or put one of her Spanish combs through it, or told her some little things such as that chicory is an adulterative in coffee. But no, I let her rave.

That hatpin prodded her. It turned out not to be a hat-pin at all but a pair of shoes that had got stolen by a tinker woman from the window-sill where they were put to dry. The sergeant traced them for her and found that they had been sold for three and elevenpence and the matter went to court. In the court, the purchaser, a creamery manager's wife, perjured herself, got flummoxed, and said she thought the tinker woman was a travelling saleswoman. The judge lit into her and gave a lecture about the sixth and seven Commandments. Lil said the scarifying bit was when she had to go up on the rostrum and identify the said shoes. According to her they looked wretched because of not having been dusted, let alone polished and buffed. She said she would have done anything to have wiped them with the nap of her coat, and have the case quashed. The culprit got a month in the county jail. 'And I in dread of peelers' she said over and over again. It had gnawed into her, that crime, that cruelty, like the rats that gnawed behind the wainscotting in Bruges or Brussels or wherever I had made that dastard journey with my spouse, Dr Flaggler. I should have embraced her, praised her for her good deeds, but I didn't. Maybe I didn't want to. She rose, or at least she attempted to rise, held on to the brass rung, tried to heft herself up, ordered the pony to be tackled, asked to be taken out of the stifling room, to the slopes of yellow gorse, to pick blackberries. She begged to come back from death's door. She mouthed it. She stopped mouthing it. Then it was so simple, so hideously simple, like the shutters going up on a big house once the season is over. It was not at all like the thing called death, it was like she was being carted, being borne in, in, in, to elsewhere, to nowhere. When I held her then, it was like holding a giant vegetable marrow. The absence of pulse and heart-beat changes everything. We did the thing with the pennies and ordered a brown shroud.

We put ourselves to the task of clearing and cleaning.

She left no heirlooms, only a fan, her ring and a little reticule. There was Boss and I. He sat by the fire, and the cries that emitted from him were not cries he was aware of. He didn't refer to her directly but kept recalling her contemporaries, girls with oaken hair, her murdered brother, blind Dr Rath. He said blind Dr Rath was a grand fellow and a great sport, had organized card games and had once put up his own table as a stake and lost it, a dining-room table, arbutus.

'You'll stay,' he said. I knew it would come but not as swiftly as that. I was not ready. I baulked. Why hadn't they died together, the way each succeeding pair of dogs had done. I donned her brown astrakhan coat and set out on foot. I walked fields, then more fields, to a river and back. An uneventful walk, apart from the pondering. Heaps of stones, great galleries of stones to the sky, to the pissing heavens, rows upon rows of stone walls and kilns. Whereas the Egyptians made pyramids. The prevailing colour was grey – sky, stone, hemisphere, all alike, all grey, tapwater grey. The leaves fell off, it would be more precise to say that they were ripped off, because there was nothing efficacious about the winds that day. Then they got themselves tagged on to some sharp point, a spike or a stump or a barb of wire. I saw it all, the future, his spleen, the humours, going coursing, on the batter, his suits having to be soaked, then the recuperation, water bottles, powders, tisanes, and along with all that, the daily rages, the cabalistic outbursts. I could not, Dodge City or no Dodge City.

When I got back to the house he was sleeping on the bedchair. He had taken a draught, the beaker was beside him, stained brown from valerian. I packed so that he would know what he had to know before being told it formally. The suitcase was down by the hall door, along with some bullrushes that I had picked.

'You shite you,' he said. After he had closed the door I heard the upper and the lower bolts snap into place.

I see the animal starting up in people, first it is a paw, then the entire tendon of a leg that goes striped and furry, and the eyes, those soft savage instruments glint with a mania of murderous yellow. In such situations I look away. Would to God I were a knitter because in such situations I could knit, or better still crochet.

A feather. It has been irking me for some time, but I have managed to wrench it from the ticking. It is fawn in colour. The feather of whom, of what. I twirl it and it responds. I blow on it, and it responds. Nice when something responds.

If I squint in a certain way I can make the wallpaper sag, so that it is swinging back and forth, with the sway of a cradle. Then I open my eyes and I see it, stark. Very intrusive. The curtains match it but they have a chintz finish. Both have for design flocks of long-tailed birds. The tails of these numerous birds trail away and are inclined to be curly and some tails loop into other tails provocatively. The owners must have had a craze for nature, or else for the shoot, shooting game. It is not a balming sight. Sometimes these birds appear to be pecking away at the paper and likewise at the chintz. Gobbling it up. Pecking instead of singing or chirping or letting out their age-old mating calls. I think the reason I haven't slept is Nick. Never occurred to me that he'd come back, that I'd got under his skin. When he came this place was in utter darkness, not a light, not even a nightlight, not even a taper. I had gone for a longer walk than usual, feeling a bit venturesome for no reason at all. I was very keen to see a sunset or a bonfire or something like that. Disastrous. First I went to a housing estate. Terrible pebbledash houses. No frames around the windows. Windows that opened straight out on to the world like gashes. I could see into every house. That shook me. Dolls and dogs and more dolls and more dogs and perambulators and children. Too many children. Napkins drying. A bit of geranium in a yoghurt carton. That grieved me. Next thing I came upon a shepherd whose crook was aluminium and only three feet long. I hankered for the time when shepherds' crooks were six feet long. Baa. Baa. Not that I've ever nabbed a sheep by the hind legs to shear him or demaggot him or do anything else with him, all twaddle, all my eye. His wife was envisaging a holiday. She was cutting out coupons to help towards a holiday, to the moors the year after next. Also they breed trout.Then they trap them and dispatch them to France where they are a delicacy of the French cuisine. It all adds up, the coupons, the pebbledash estate, the packets of cereal with cardboard clocks on them, the dolls in the window, their legs splayed, the dolls as grotesque as the children. Went as far as Mortlake to a cemetery. Then I lay on a hillside, pleurisy-making for sure, and saw the dark coming on, and the very odd thing about the oncoming dark was that it was as if my own eyes were failing me. Everything began to go blur. There was nothing thrilling in the way of a new moon or a full moon or even a curlew curlewing. There was nothing at all only the dark coming down, like a cloth at the extremities of the world, grey, dun, and the near things visible though not discernible and the hub of the traffic somewhere beyond. As soon as the ground felt damp to the touch, I rose to wend my way. It took me a long time what with going astray and all that. Murder entered my mind, or beheading, or a rosy crucifixion. I had to cross a common and there wasn't a soul except myself and a runner in a track suit, threshing through the ferns. All this walking, there must be some purpose to it, I said to myself, coming in at the gate that creaked. I dare say all gates creak unless they get treated to linseed oil from time to time.

There it was waiting for me, half in, half out of the letterbox. I rushed into the hall, and then, as always with portents, I hesitated before unsealing it. 'In votre absence

Nick came.' I dropped, I almost snivelled. Missed a nice fuck. We would have been shy at first, but maybe we would have come out of our shells and started kissing in the dark, and feeling as in an undergrowth, then reclining, our persons buoyed up on beautiful blue plush, no missus of his to disquiet us, him telling me little things and I retaliating, and everything between us verdant and radiant with promise. We might have danced an old-time waltz. Nothing in the world to equal it for harmony, for concinnity as they say. I would have made him a little snack. Damnation to it.

Paramours are not battering on any door, there's no form at the casement saying 'I'm waiting for you love'. I can't cavil. I've had my share, even a lumberman from Scandia with a very radical thrust. A motley crew, all shades, dimensions, breeds, ilks, national characteristics, inflammatingness, and penetratingness. Some randy, many conventional, one decrepit. An old man. He couldn't bear the ticking of my bedside clock. I could smell death and extreme unction off him. Why did I concur? An act of clemency, one of my very few. He was a Benjaminite. I couldn't do that now. Farcical. Rather a cowhorn, or a thornbush through the arse. Harrowing that was called in Coose, that impact of thornbush on obstinate land. That was before machinery. That was before.

Machines have played their part in my life too. Machines and people. Perfidious. People cling on to me like sloths. How they weigh, how they prey upon me. I am prepared to vouchsafe that they are attached to my scalp by means of brooches, so tenacious are they. I am amazed at the number of people that can be affixed to a normal-sized scalp. I take size nine in a hat. Sometimes they surpass themselves, get rowdy, boisterous, take to swinging back and forth like children or bantams, upon a fender or a swing gate at eventide. I was ever one for eventide. I have so many maudlin memories of it, the soft feel of wallflowers, or is it heliotrope, showers of rain, smoke curling up, the dogs famished, mavourneen, the pig badgers and the dog badgers out, warring, evening auguring towards night, and such a momentum of tears, and for what, and for whom – Lil, Boss, Dr Flaggler, Tutsie.

Nick was of the red-haired fraternity, and growing a beard. We danced, divinely. The floor was sheer. I would like to think that our bloodstreams danced, bounced, bounded together. I would like to think our sensibilities met. Is that possible? Melted into one another. Suddenly his wife was there, prancing about like an old lioness. She was a dab hand at it, prancing. She nudged him with her shoulder, then bumpsie daisy with one of her flanks, then ousting me out of place she tried levering herself on to him. There was a touch of a dancer or a stripper about her. A bit of a trouper. She started to undress. He commenced on my necklaces, started untugging. The lights were lowered but the music put up. We were no longer dancers, we were performers, three, at each other, at. She bayed like a hyena. He flicked her in the air and unerringly she came down. Well trained, a trapeze artist, a wife. Conceited slaves. Come to think of it she was not like an old lioness, she had more in common with a washing board, bleached, scoured, dry. He moved us towards their tossed bed. He mimed to her what to do. She went to a medicine cabinet. She had to coax it open with her nail as the key was missing and there was no little latch or handle for her benefit. She scooped some cream out of a blue tin. It was white and over-runny, and I was able to recall the exact price of it, and knew that a hundred lids of that commodity could secure a plastic tulip for some town housewife with a yen for the forest. She was no forest woman, more your allotment ilk. Comes, half comes, quarter comes, struggles at comes, they are much the same thing. We battled and wrestled and slept and wakened and adhered and writhed, throughout the night. His snores had a trace of mucus in them.

'Hark, he said, 'the house awakens.' I heard of all things a baby cry, such an ordinary, no, such an extraordinary thing. It seems to me that babies along with cows are passing from our lives altogether. Soon they will be after-images, cords, threads, suspenders, emanations, suspenders to former times. I slipped away. Quite united they looked, he half awake, she feigning sleep or maybe it only seemed to be a feign because of the way her lids trembled, maybe dreaming she was, roguish dreams. Travelling home in my dishevelled state I met nuns and milkmen. It was a Sunday. The nuns were muttering their prayers and the milkmen doing their rounds. Long white notes protruded from empty milk bottles. Probably they were for alternative orders – double cream for the jellies, brown eggs for Grandma, a cancellation maybe. I was not in any hurry. I was dressed in lamé of all things and the air was to my liking, drizzly.

I wouldn't mind living it all over again. I met them in the pub where there was a sort of improvised ball. Phil the Fluter stuff. It was New Year's Eve, and just at midnight people jumped up and started to dance and to rout other people out of their chairs. The hard topers spit in their drinks to put their bespoke on them. I'd gone there alone for a decko. Amazing enticements – speed, lights, food, chicks, disc jockeys and table telephones. It was like the eve of Waterloo all of a sudden, that so-called spiffing night when Belgium's capital gathered her beauty and her chivalry. There we were, linking, moving *en masse* to the gallery, one faction going up the steps, and another bursting out into the street and little side groups weaving their way between tables, weaving and waving, concertina music, baritone voices, the mirrors frosted, the dun pillars skewered with masks, the whole place alive with singing and gaudiness, people catching sight of themselves and making weird faces and blowing kisses. There was no resident band but the regulars had brought their own instruments – spoons, combs, penny whistles. There were plenty of Coose spalpeens in that *mêlée* but I shunned them, it was Nick I tagged on to. 'Tap o' the mornin' to you,' he said.

'To hell or to Connaught,' I said, using the war cry of Oliver Cromwell.

'Don't go away,' he said, touching my buttoned bodice. Something nice about him, a softie. I could picture him with a slane, cutting turf and chewing his quid of tobacco, with maybe a pipe, a hubbly bubbly or a cherry-wood to gnash on. I suppose osmosis was our first actual endeavour, the sucking came later when we rammed through into the garden of life, and the gnashing came with the teeth. I spent the night with him and his spouse, we scrambled upstairs after closing time. They were managers there, which meant we had free nuts, free booze and the companionship of their guard dog, an Alsatian, a eunuch, named Boris.

'Come here you git and fetch this fucking coal,' she said.

As master of the house he insisted on making a fire to ring out the old and ring in the new. Lucky he didn't burn her smalls that were drying on a chair.

'Slag,' he said, as she hefted the coal across the floor; and he asked the Fates how long were they married. A lifetime he said.

'Still, we had a good time last night, didn't we?' she said, bold as brass. Not lacking in gumption. Men like women to do their warring for them. The canny Scythians choose to use their mares in warre service rather than their stone horses. She proceeded to dish up a late dinner, a mutton hash, without deference to me. The upshot was he gave me his, she gave him hers, while she ate directly from the casserole. To her I was more or less invisible, simply not there. That was prior to our debauch. But as things warmed up and he filled my glass until it foamed over, she took cognizance of me, she admired my hairstyle, but said to make no mistake about it, that she came first, that she was number one, that she was Mrs Finney. He told her for fuck's sake to belt up.

'I might let you have him,' she said, 'I don't particularly want him, except for his balls now and then.' She asked where I got my clothes, my couture. She said she would have considered modelling except that she was into the breeding racket, big deal, ha ha ha. It seems they had four children, none of whom I saw and only one of whom I heard. A mewl.

Nick's wife has another ruse, another bit of hen-pecking, she insists Nick carry a wad of notes in case they are suddenly discharged from their posts as managers, in case they must flee, and then, because he is in possession of such exorbitant sums, it stands to reason, he can't have a stroll alone, he has to be escorted by her or by the tiddleywinks. I wouldn't like to tread on her corns again.

In the morning she was loath to let him see me out. She told me to get my own fucking taxi and hitch up with my own man. She doesn't know that I like guerrillas, men on the move, stonemasons like Moriarty, and a volunteer called McKann. I only know Mc Kann by hearsay but I often think he's the one, the destiny for me. I saw photos of him, very still and mild, like a crock of milk, and yet he burns with a fierce indignation like a burning bush. I might meet him in the woods, in Arcadia.

I am reaching for the pushbell. Imagine that for an amenity. There is even a fireplace here and fire-irons and a basket grate. It is a boudoir. There is a love seat. Just before rain the soot falls. The gales are in fits and starts, a sum of all the gales from all the chimneys in the world, Coose, Alaska, the unpeopled climes. The soot makes a scurrying sound like mice marching. Sometimes in half sleep I imagine that it is mice and that they have got into a boot or my suède and are lying there in ambush. In the mornings I gather up the soot on a piece of cardboard. No rain tonight but a storm brewing. Marvellous feeling, as if everything in nature is going to erupt. I might end up in China or Tasmania. Without even looking I can tell what it is like outside in the garden, very grave though blowy, the big dark trees towering, the magnificent sweep of the lawns, everything pointing towards the stars and everything rooted but by no means reconciled. Now if it were a summer's night I might don a shawl and have a stroll out there and when summer comes I shall and will. I pity those at sea. It's so nice to be here, installed, snug. I would ring this cursed pushbell except that I cannot bear the denouement. It is not going to be answered, no flunkey is going to rush up here with smelling salts or camomile tea, and say 'Yes, ma'am,' or 'No, ma'am'. It is white, cold and sphere-shaped and I expect that it has a little battery inside it. I touch it and suddenly it is ringing me and my fingers are pins and needles and the electricity is getting to my palm. I drop it and repair to the far side of the bed. It is now on a pillow abandoned. This side of the bed is freezing and unfriendly.

The thing I hanker after is custard, great soft glaubs of it in the mouth, not too sweet, but certainly with a dash of vanilla. A harmless mush, feeble under the impact of mastication, perfect at sliding down. No chewing, no wrestle. Into the kitchen. I rummage. There are seven varieties of soup and these have ingredients that are positively epicurean – oyster, crab, game, goose, tomato, celeriac, and turtle. There is a substance called glutamate added, which casts aspersions on the whole thing. I do not know this glutamate, I am not familiar with its properties, it could give bouquet but then again it could vanquish the game, the goose, the oyster, the turtle, the

celeriac and so on. Poor bread has gone mouldy, it is
furred and swollen. I bought it three days ago. It had
cellophane around it that I ripped off on the way home
and bit into it, warm, and fresh as it was, straight from
the bakery. Now it's black, with inlays of green. The fur
has the glisten of sea salt, looks as if it might bristle but it
can't, it is only bread, forgotten bread. I have not the will
to bite into it or maul into it so I say good-bye by closing
the enamel lid with a fierce thud. Next to the soups there
are spices but all have lost their pungency because of the
damp. They rigged the thermostat to make it as cool as
possible. I invariably walk around in a blanket except
when some beau is coming, then I get into my finery, my
voile or my chiffon. They would be appalled now to come
into their own kitchen, things higgledy-piggledly, delf
unwashed, tea leaves in a saucepan, and the carrier bags
with the retailers' names on them, scattered round. We
have weevils. It is easy to tell by the way the crumbs, the
crumbs of water biscuit, are scattered. Some crumbs are
white, but most are a scorched brown because it is high-
baked biscuits I asked for in the shop. The man in the
shop squeezed my hand when giving me the change,
called me Dusty. 'You made my day,' he said. Probably
says it to everyone. More power to his elbow. I don't
patronize the supermarkets, I prefer the shops where I
can talk to the assistants and get their histories.

I often think that the heart I am possessed of is a little
chicken's heart, a little pullet's, maybe a White Wyan-
dotte's or a crossbreed, maybe that is why Lil coddled me,
because I reminded her of her favourite thing, her prize
poultry. Thread the needle, thread the needle. Lil was
champion at knots and quipus, had brought it to a fine
art, the crafty old Druids knot, intricate as the Coose
snaim.

The earliest milk she gave me was from a bottle, later a
vessel. The cows were my friends, even though we had no
rapport. We shat in the same places, that is to say the

hills and the dales, the lambent meadows of Coose, in random places, under trees and not under trees, we were not very fastidious. The circumference of theirs larger, richer, and more grandiose than mine, a man-sized shoe could sink into theirs and still be outdone, outdistanced that is. Cows concern me. The world's hide, the world's blameless udder. I would have stayed near to them in the ark, mingled their breaths with mine. I still champion them and it is not because of my watchstrap either, or my pampooties, or my morning milk that laces my morning tea. But I have a feeling that they are disappearing from our lives altogether. I shall miss them, I shall pine. That is one of my propensities. I would have been great in the heyday of the Greek times, propped up between temples, tearing hair out and invoking the many and opposing Fates. Soon their lowing, their hides, their teats, their udders, their saunter, their curling tails, their matted tails, the dry and undry scour of their rumps, their dipping umbilical cords, soon all these will be after-images, spectres of things that we once saw at morningtide, or at eveningtide, or when on our annual vacations. Another thing, these successions of cows that I once knew still bawl in my head, as indeed do the swine and the cockerels and the kid goats and the fenny fowl and the ducks and the geese and the swans and the herons and the cranes and the coots and the didappers and the waterhens and the teals and the curs and the drakes and the sheldrakes and the peckled fowls and the flocking sheep, all, all the sirenic and the not-so-sirenic sounds that they let out at the instant of their near deaths. Not that I am a habitué of the abattoirs. On the contrary, I go to gardens, to the hothouse at Kew, for aftermaths of Coose.

Coose, that old Alma Mater. Low lying. A glorified bog. A village, village men, village women, bursts, outbursts, corn, fermentation, rot, dogs, mange, shingles, nerves, hollyhocks, sucking calves, (severed from their ma's) sucking at worn pails with jagged edges, later frisking and gambolling in paddocks; very few strangers except for an Arab who removed cataracts, and paupers who rampaged potato pits. A stark land, loamy and miry, full of rain and bleat, two bleats, man and beast, ink light inclining towards black, inclining towards mourn; by no means an oriental people. A race more mindful of waters and crinkled bladders, slack-jawed, weak in the mandibles from eating sops of hay and farinaceous matter. 'Around the house and mind the dresser!' Such were the anthems of the wild men of Coose in their marathon jigs and reels. Very pugnacious. Not a baccalaureate among them, not even a martyr for the annals. Ignoramuses who couldn't tell cheese from soap, both being hard, off-white substances and tasting of curds when placed in the mouth. Bostoons. Still, everything has its little role on the earth's surface, even the pismire and the much admired lily, even us. The Arab had a habit of beating his head upon the ground prior to removing these cataracts and cysts, calling upon his god who was not our God. He did strange rituals with his own waters and called all women sultanas. Insisted on getting paid in goods and chattles, creels of turf or grass for his camel. Another hobo, nicknamed The Birdie, a crooner, sang The Bells of St Mary's while slipping his hand in under women's clothing when they happened to be at devotions, or admiring the scenery, or exchanging their farm produce, their dairy goods for marvels such as cochineal or Oxford lunch cake. A heart-rending voice he had. People were stirred, moved to tears when he sang the ballads – even those ladies were moved to tears who had formerly been obliged to fend him off with their lashing tongues or the metal spirals of their corseting. Purity prevailed, yet lapsed. Plenty of hatch, batch and dispatch. Hatch a woefully wicked thing, done down in pits and holes and the sunkenness of wet hedges. The hawthorn was grand. A most gay and diaphanous sight in the month of May, as if Coose were going to be the location for pageantry. No such luck. Coose was Coose. No fire brigade. A midwife called Polly who was late for all her offices, late because she moved cumbrously, like an old-fashioned perambulator. Lived in the woods. She was reputed to have buff on her ceilings, and buff on her hall door, some said buff on her arse. Yet we are mentioned in the Norse books, in the *Kongs Skugo* and the *Speculum Regali*. We are not nonentities by no means.

I fled from it in the tender years, after an incident, deflowering, a botched job, a case of *coitus interruptus* if ever there was one. Took place not in a canoe or on a chaise-longue, but out in the open, with a fellow who hailed from the city, a one-night stand. It was St Peter and St Paul's day, hence a holy day of obligation. Lovely season, the latter end of June, goslings hissing across the land, the new potatoes, the swarths of new-mown hay, the frogspawn in skeins, their amber jelley peppered with its young, the odd baby frog getting dashed to pieces but such things are commonplace. It began harmlessly enough – the holy sacrament of the Mass, a snappy sermon and in the inclement afternoon, a fancy dress parade. Decked in a long frock with a chaplet of dwarfs stitched on, I presented myself as Snow White and the Seven Dwarfs. There was a glut of Snow Whites and some with a retinue of dwarfs far more convincing, such as gnomes or toddlers. Alas several little drummer boys, jockeys, Tessie O'Sheas, and bauld Fenian men. The prizewinner turned out to be none other than a brown paper parcel. A parcel, within it another, and another and another, until at the very centre, a very underfed creature came peering through, screeching. Her mother before her screeched, which is why they eventually took her to the Castle, the choice name for the loony bin. After presenting her with a prize of two china bow-wows, the carnival proper was opened – bumpers, chairoplanes,

swingboats, rifle ranges and playing machines from
Dodge City. Later an all-night hop. Packed. The Master
of the Hounds, and Mrs Hoare-O'Shaughnessy did the
Hokey Pokey for the veneration of all. Then they vanished. They were caught in some hanky panky business,
hanky between him and her, in their cod places, with him
entreating and inveighing upon her, and the galvanized
door, their mating venue, clattering and causing such
ructions as to alert a junior guard and speedy him to the
illfamed spot. A Connemara man, red-headed, intervened
with baton and with beaming torch. The news spread
like wildfire and apart from the graphic speculations
there was a consensus that the guard would get sent to
Bohatch for coming upon the gentry, married gentry at
that, in their midsummer bacchante. Little did I know
that my hour was nigh. I was dancing with a falconer, to
the strains of Sweet Rosie O'Grady, when he volunteered
the information that I had stripped a fine woman. He
was referring to the transparency of the Snow White attire. He said that the prizewinner, Miss Kitty O'Screechy,
had got it out of pull. He said to be warned, that everything in Coose was got out of pull – pensions, gun li-
cences, agricultural grants, everything. He asked would I
click. I said 'Click click' as I had seen Americans do with
box cameras. Then the crooner jumped down from the
bandstand, it being his supper break, walked straight
across and said 'Excuse me, Angel.' Very suave, fawn suit,
crêpe-soled shoes, a dicky bow and so forth. Kept saying
Swell. I was in clover. Said would I care for a blow. A
nice night out, bats, summer moths, everything sultry as
in the land of Spain; Boss and Lil safely at home reciting
the Rosary. He said where would we go, I said anywhere.
Had a knack of tickling the palm, featherish, much more
adroit than the Coose men. We headed for the limestone
rock, the town's beauty spot. He lost no time, got his belt
undone, said 'I could go through you like butter.' Suc-
cussive sounds. He started to slaver. His proboscis, his

front feeder looking for its trough. Gush gush. Niagara Falls. I dodged it. Niagara, partly on me, but chiefly on limestone rock and as I imagined, getting into the fissures, either nourishing or nauseating the lichen, the sphagnum, the roots of the tree, and the various insects and night creatures that were reposing there. Destitute of all words he was, except 'swell'. Abrupt termination. 'You go first, I'll follow' and he skedaddled off to the commercial hotel to get a bite of supper. Didn't ask if I had a mouth on me. Tooraloo. They were playing Jealousy when I got back and a twitess called Dolly, his stand-in, was singing at the top of her voice. She was wearing a cerise dress and the spotlights were leaping all over her. That's who I wanted to be, Dolly. Crossing the floor at a moment when it happened to be a ladies' choice, I bumped into a hunchback, one of those water diviners – who due either to perversity or gormlessness, said 'Yes with knobs on' and launched into a murderous caterbrall. He said it didn't take long, me and the jackeen, that it was a brusque affair. Not very *au fait* with the facts of life and bred on the melodrama. I began to get a touch of morning sickness even though it was bordering on midnight. I foresaw things, amplification of the event, cudgels, the ecclesiastical intervention and opprobrium from within the bosom of the family. So I decided to make myself scarce. I took a night boat to the land across water, to get cacodemonised as Lil would say if she were on earth, and asked for an opinion.

I don't know anyone who hasn't grown up in a madhouse, whose catechising hasn't been Do this, Do that, Don't do this, Do do it, I'll cut the tongue out of you, How bloody dare you, D'you hear? I said don't do it, Do do it, Sing, Vocalize, Belt up, Blow your nose, Stop picking that nose, Piss, Eat your pandy, Stop making that noise, Who farted? No farting, Don't shit, you shit you.

*

Among the foe. The Brits, the painted people. A land where the king has piles. Not much resonance to it. Sportsmen, huntsmen, sportswomen abound. Fanatic at following the hunt, these ladies chasing the bushy-tailed foxes, by no means genteel, by no means porcelain, not renowned for their cornucopias. Royalty make a big to-do about meeting at galas and regattas – a king, a queen, aunts, grandaunts, sons, and daughters, nieces, nephews, blood cousins, half cousins, ladies-in-waiting, occasional people, all nicely accoutred. I see photos of them. I like to study their hair styles and try out their deportment, I am very impressed with their deportment and their low starch diets which I read of in the magazines. These I read for free. There is a resting hall where I go and where I can lounge for hours with no one to evict me. Sometimes other people – natterers – try to start up a conversation with me about their boilers or the generation gap or the foul weather, but I pretend to be a Norwegian. I like that ruse, pretending to be a captain's daughter, a captain void of feelings, always looking through his binoculars, looking out to sea and swaying on solid land. I can even avail of a little morsel for free because in the shop proper they are always plugging a soup or a *pâté* or a brand of biscuit and I take my place in the queue along with all the esteemed. Then back for another read or a daydream as the case may be. The only thing that mars the full bliss of it is that I am perpetually afraid that people are going to trip over me. I have the impression that there is some valuable inside of me that's going to get dislodged and fall out if I am crashed into. It must be my jumping jack or my gut. In the photos the royalty are always exchanging handshakes and smiling, even though it is obvious that they have only just parted at their own portals. I am always home before the rush hour. Then I sit for a while, giving thanks. From the back window I have a view of four gas chimneys and in some lights they look yellow and threaten to taper into the air.

The smoke that puffs out is as ambling as clouds. The clouds here are dull and hefty. They don't roam the way they did in Coose. There are roses, winter roses, pinpoints, high on a bed of foliage, rusted, rotting, unkempt roses, still they bloom and are hanging on. I have even considered making a pot pourri. It will be a talking point if I invite people here, but I will need a utensil, a skull or a glass bowl, or a perforated pan into which to put these petals, and sepals and achenes, and ovaries and stamens and husks and calyxes and ovules and follicles and stipules, not forgetting the merry hips, the merry haws. The guests will smell, then dip their fingers or their snouts in, make little reshuffles, say exclamatory things, that is if I do it, and if I have guests.

I used to know hosts of people. One in particular stands out – one Maurice P. Moriarty and I saw many a night through, loquacious in our cups, bent over the embers, bemoaning our limestone kilns, our lineage and so forth. Moriarty's family had a walnut tree, a genus Juglans from Persia. He used to say, 'If it weren't for a thing called love, I'd love *you*.' Thank you. Abdul Abulbul Abee. Moriarty had freckles on his balls which goes to show what a mandarin he was. I used to cart him to his bed. We never consummated it. It was about the best there was, I mean the most rending apart from the bloodknots. It was more of a boneknot. Down with bloodknots, boneknots, Minoan knots, Tristram knots, Druidic knots and Lil's spittled-on speciality, the mother's knot.

He came to dwell for a bit. Worked on a building site, immunised himself to the noise. He used to bring four bottles of stout and station them on the kitchen table, two each. We used to imagine scaffolds for each other, places where we would scale and occasionally meet. It probably got too much for him, it probably got to be a bit of a rope around his neck.

He left without saying farewell. He went out to get cigarettes from a machine when the shades of night were down, and lo and behold, he did not come back. He might have met someone or else he hijacked himself to the desert. He was always on about the desert, the scorching, the nomads and so forth. I would say he met someone, a girl, bleached, straw-like, his type. Maybe Sharon, the one that came here. Couldn't tell the difference between swallowing and chewing, or rather, she was unable to fix the delineating moment and to decide when to desist from one and commence upon the other. It deluded her so that from her earliest years she chewed and swallowed indiscriminately, and knew the correctness of her actions only as it was registered by others who in their turn praised, scolded or pounded her for what she had just unwittingly done. I was addled with her, what with her reminiscence and her cooing and her eating habits. When eating a chocolate biscuit she grazed the chocolate off the biscuit, grazed it, then licked it, then dived into the biscuit proper. She had beautiful features but no beauty, it is often the case. One day she brought me a present of nougat, nice of her. Moriarty used to employ his time drawing stars, blue-black, very jagged stars, done in ink and though he never looked at her, they were meant for her. She thought they were scrumptious.

Ah well, the Moriartys of this world are on some bier.

Of course other people do come here and for the most motley and comical reasons; to deliver a pamphlet or a plaster, to collect the church dues, to put the wickerwork back in the chairs, to sharpen the knives, to maintenance the carpets, or to inform me that I have won a mystery prize of twopence, frequently to beg. I have no bloodhounds to set upon them, so I vary the means by which I can get rid of them. I feign deaf and dumb. I slam the door. I palliate. I shout down from an upstairs window that I have a curling tongs to my hair. A very nice man came to mend a gas leak and because of having to strike matches to relight the pilot lights, he put the four used matches back into his own box so as not to defile my kitchen, their kitchen. Now I call that thoughtful, don't you? I wouldn't have minded a walk with him, in the twilight, a bit of handholding, fingers plaiting, all that. He looked like a star gazer, absorbed and remote.

'Have a sherry,' I said. We drank it standing up. He was shy, not like most of those gadflies who try to get in if you're in a negligée or a shift, keep peering at you around the pap region. One such felon snapped at my dressing-gown braid and said 'Hi, Freckles.' Freckles! I am as white as calico and have only been exposed to extreme sunshine twice in my life. I'm wary of beggars, being mindful of the Coose saw about vagrants who die leaving fortunes in their scapulars. Some I bring in, for consolation, or a preamble, some for a fuck. The waiter for instance. There are times when our limbs make our decisions for us. Quite a sniper he was. Tight trousered. His dangle brought me to considering him, that and his ferocious impertinence. Not even a head waiter, a flunkey, throwing platters down and then waiting to be told thank you in a foreign Erse. Insisted I eat snails, I who lack co-ordination with any kind of implement. Made my escort, who is a mock duke, and allergic to shellfish, have a lobster thermidor. Poor man was obliged to spend the bulk of the ensuing time over a washbasin. The waiter, finding himself unimpeded, removed his striped apron so that I could have a better view of him, à la hips, pelvis, and groin. There he was, aiding and abetting himself in a too-tight trousers. The plans for our liaison got completed in ten seconds. He bowed when we were leaving and called me madam. The Duke had to appropriate one of their pink linen napkins lest the jogging of the taxi induce another bout. He couldn't understand why I didn't drop in and stroke his forehead, do a bit of palming as we called it. That was one of my favours, that and donning suspenders, in return for which I got treats, dinners, bunches of flowers and numerous little bottles of bath essence. I had to feign a migraine and hurried home.

I thought of him and his preen. It didn't matter the colour or how pimpled or how tufted, or how pink or how ochre or how egalitarian or how distended or how not. I went around the house tidying, crooning, said 'A lover is coming,' sang it, then did exercises to get into a more strapping condition. He arrived, wearing smoke-blue sunglasses in this a winter solstice. He sat on the pouffe. If there had been a cheetah he would have sat on that. He sought to impress. He mentioned blue blood and Botticelli, and frescoes on bathroom ceilings. He said he would drink anything I drank, he would drink my words. First major setback. Then a most hideous development. He started on about the vicissitudes of fortune. His life story, his poverty, his growing pains, long years of apprenticeship, his culinary courses, getting double-crossed; and in his immediate circumstances having to miss the bus home each night due to the thoughtlessness of customers who dallied. It seems they dallied more after they were served some liquor that he had to set fire to, some colourless liquor strewn with coffee beans. He said some of them were so drunk that they aspired to eat the flames, especially the ladies, scalding themselves, their tongues and their tonsils; crying out for ointment and jellies, asking him to be a first-aid man. Lo, and behold, a sadder tale. His room was cold, his walls were damp and devoid of pictures or engravings, he had no wardrobe and only two metal hangers. He was in possession of an oil heater but forbore from lighting it before he went out in the morning because he had read of numerous catastrophes concerning oil heaters and families of small children. I was waiting for news of chilblains. I made a serious attempt to thwart him. I flung questions at him, questions pertaining to the libido. I said 'What is your type, do you like it straight or sausage, do you like rubber goods?' He droned on. Yes, he had had girl friends and the sequence of relationships was that he acted chivalrous on the first occasion, gave them their kicks; on the second occasion satisfied himself and on the third and fourth, picked for a fight. Picked. I looked down at his fingernails and received a most inglorious shock. One nail was black and had grown inordinately, and as far as I could gauge had grown soft, was nearer to flesh than to horn. Alas for the little preparations upstairs, the whip placed strategically on the bedspread, the black whip, the white bedspread, the ovoid of soap, yellow as egg yolk. The whip was a gift from a beady-eyed lady, a Lebanese, who had said 'You might like to hang it in your bathroom.' I thought to hell with repugnance, we will wend our way upstairs, and do something, yoga if necessary. I poured toddies of a spirit made from Swedish grain, oats as far as I can remember. I smiled, pursed lips, dilated the pupils, all that. But the nails intervened, the yellowing nails and the one black soft one. His *savoir-faire* decreased as his life story unfurled. It is ever thus. He spoke of his father, deceased. He said not to have a father was a lonesome thing. I could have contested that but didn't. He had come with one set of thoughts and intentions and suddenly, hark, his father's death loomed. I could strangle myself for inducing sentiment. It was all so predictable, the rigmarole, how his father had grown thin throughout his long illness but that immediately after his death his cheeks puffed out so that as a corpse he was a credit to them. Peasants. The more he talked the more I felt myself turning into a sponge, no, not a sponge, but a stone, dry, hard, obdurate; a pumice stone through which nothing seeped, not even a scrap of pity. His life, his tatty little life was taking shape on me as it was told. I got fidgety. I saw his dangle drop into the dust. I gave voice to sympathy but the think I couldn't endure was the third finger of the right hand. The nail was not only soft, not only black, but it seemed to be sprouting, elongating before my very eyes. First the nail repelled me, then the finger, then the hand, then the wrist and gradually the repulsion spread and his farts filled the room, putrefied the atmosphere, brought on my customary choking. His farts were the deadliest of all, made up one had to ask, of what things; what roots, plants, gristles, and victuals had gone into him? Other people's dishes, sampled on the way in, other people's leavings gobbled on the way out. Suddenly I leapt up, offered him money, a forfeit, restitution, told him that he had to go, vamoose, skip it, that he was endangered, that a lover, a gangster, hovered with cuttle bones, that his young life was in danger, to go, to please go, to go, and have the sacrament of the mass offered for his dead father, to find a young girl, a Tuscany girl, one of his own. It was not as easy as that, the very rebuffs he relished. I tried to drive him from the place, this place. He knelt, he crawled, he imprecated, he dribbled, he slobbered. Kneeling he nuzzled. How identical our debasements are. He begged for me to just hold it, said he would come and that would be that. Alas for that prognostication. A small emission followed, not very gravant, and with a most spattery sound. It could not have been ghastlier. I cleaned and scoured and with a hairdryer attended to the Moroccan pouffe.

I expect someone died in this room. I heard hymns once. I have parted the curtains in order to be a watchdog. To see the moon if it should saunter by. Another of my slaveries, even though it be a mere secondary planet, another of my fixations, on a par with my liking for the shadows and the birds and the hermits. I understand there are bird squads, commandos with fumes and searchlights to send them back into the wilderness. May God wither up their hearts, may their blood cease to flow ...

It is dark, inside and out, but the hour will come when the black light will stubbornly give way to a grey and then to a greyish blue and maybe at last, towards morn-

ing, near the aurorate, a pink or orange light will invade
the heavens and it will for a moment or a series of
moments disseminate itself and I will see a lit-up pane,
burnished, and say to myself all is not lost, all is not
bleak, and the heavens and the earth can still spring their
little surprises on me and flood the world with radiance.
Tower of ivory, house of gold. And the pigeons under the
eaves will coo. And I will laugh or I will cry. There is
little difference. What more do I want.

I am here in the capacity of a caretaker. They needed
someone to take in the mail and douche the plants and so
forth. Also to turn on lights in the evening, to give the
semblance of a full house. They are irrational about being robbed. They ply me with post-cards saying they hope
they haven't been you-know-whated. Antelopes roaming
the ranges. I keep a blunderbuss on the chiffonier, hoping that the sight of it, plus my sagging tits plus my oat-
meal mask, will offset any rude assailant. I might carouse
with him or suggest a game of Sardines. All it needs is for
him to be a certain type, a sort of defunct hangman,
granite featured, for me to get into the swing of it, get the
old hairy scutcheons sliding, get on with the Thigh Show.

Needless to add I appropriated the master bedroom,
the electric blanket and this quilt. The room they as-
cribed to me was a single room with red wallpaper, of the
oxblood variety. Lil had the audacity to appear there one
night, swaddled in linen no less, and with a rosary swinging from her waist. The curtains lifted as if a flame or a
breeze had been put to them and there she was, rouged,
rejuvenated. Full of wise saws about Jesus, whom she
called Jesu. I found it an impertinence myself. She had
little gold sleepers in her ears. Some goddam dreg of love
welled up in me and I wanted to put my hand out and
touch the earlobe, the cool, the white earlobe that just
missed being chafed by the rim of the gold. I wanted to
tweak it. At the same time I wished she'd make herself
scarce and said so. She was sermonizing in her customary

voice, about the joys of heaven and the writhing woes of hell. I wanted to inquire into the statute acreage of same and also to ask if unfortunate children got born there. She kept limbo and purgatory out of the narrative altogether. I could smell the sizzling and the burning of flesh from the great tale with which she regaled me. So vivid was it that I could see them, these poor souls, rotomating like chickens, as I've seen and watched them in the takeaway 'Nosh' place. She was looking very august. To tell you the truth her visitation gave me the willies. I was afraid she might nake herself. I was digging into the mattress and sweating like a pig. She actually got into the bed, the single bed. It squeaked. I edged away. Who wouldn't. She arched and tilted and bowed her body so that she fitted exactly into mine, my tumescence and my curves, her tumescence and her curves, and it felt as if we were being welded together, or at least moulded together, like one of her legendary carragheen soufflés in its wetted mould. She had precepts written out on a slate, in gold no less, like the Writ of Moses, stipulating further how I must live out the remainder of my life. She kept adhering to me. Such suctorial sounds, such busying. Then she started to infer that she would be resident here for all time, keeping a total watch. She was not like Hamlet's father, coming back at an appointed hour to deliver State news or instigate a bit of foul play. She was going to be trailing me for the rest of my life, counting the number of cigarettes I smoked, my alcoholic intake, the knaves that I brought home, my femoral moments with the Duke, she was to be my guardian angel. I had the most terrible feeling, the most shocking realization, you cannot kill the dead. And yet I had a go, in fact I wakened up howling and aiming the warming pan at her. I gathered up my effects.

This room is brighter as well as airier and the bed itself is on a dais. The pictures and gouaches are the backs or buttocks of various Japanese ladies. It seems he has a preference for backs, so Tig said. The wardrobes are louvred and the drawers inhumanly neat, along with being lavender-scented. There are also camphor balls volleying back and forth at the merest wrench, and I gainsay that they are the genuine thing from Borneo. In my cups I mistook them for sweets and bit into one, expecting a peppermint bouquet. Recently the place has suffered a bit of wear and tear. A table that I broke has been removed from sight. I simply locked the door, took the key and on my forenoon walk dropped it into the little pond where there are splints of ice and where there is also reputed to be carp, John Dorys, bleak and bream. It was a fiendish room, a dining-room, a morgue, twelve high-backed chairs, a perspex hotplate, artificial fruits which I hazard to say were not unlike artificial testicles. I dine in the kitchen, perch on a high stool. The saucepans are gleaming. I have looked at myself in the bottom of those saucepans and my reflection is positively fulgent. I like it here. Of course it is not ideal, but it is a resting place. The silences are unnerving. I can hear my own hair splitting. Very often as I go down the stairs, the swish of my skirt surprises me and causes me to start as if I am about to be given a clout of some kind. Another thing I hear is the salt as it falls on to my food, that little shiver it gives as I sprinkle it on to the forkful of cabbage or whatever I happen to be eating. I am a devil for cabbage. I wouldn't mind a few beds of York cabbage in the rose garden and my having to go out with my spray gun and stop the slugs from mottling it, and eating right through, to the bunch that is its heart. Then there are the other things, the senseless sounds, the creaks, maybe worms in the futtocks and timbers, or maybe it's the timbers themselves settling down or revolting after hundreds of years. They are not exactly musical, but no one is asking them to be. I recall that the sweetest note I ever heard was the rupture of a cobweb as it tore, scattered and fell. Jewelled it was from the sun and shaped like a mandala. It was in a boilhouse in Coose. In the breach the note sounded, and then the silence sounded. I don't know why it got torn, as there was no reason for it, no fist or no slashhook, but it did. It may have decided to give up.

I am getting used to my own company, my own dissertations. I play Patience, play variations on it. It is then that the long grey tenders of cigarette-ash burn their way into some item of furniture and I jump up, my mouth full of apologies. I shall be busy with the turps, one day, one day.

Maybe I should not have come here, maybe it has given me a taste for reverie. I should have gone as a dairymaid or a lady's companion, or even a gentleman's companion. But it was glorious the morning I applied. It was autumn time, a beautiful bronze light, the birch leaves like sovereigns, the wide granite steps sweeping up to the house, the two pushbells and a policeman strolling around, overseeing all. Inside, everything sunny, everything tinkling, chimes and so forth, and when I looked up at the big high ceilings and the cornices I foresaw myself giving hoolies and suppers. The first thing I did when I came to reside was to make myself familiar with the light switches. I know these switches off by heart. I dare say I know them better than they do. For instance, on one of the landings there is an array of switches that operates lights above and below even as far down as the cellar, and I can go to any one of these switches and be certain of which it is I am turning on. I practised it for nights on end and would go up and down to see the correctness or otherwise of my actions. In the case of the cellar I had to stoop and see the crack of light under the door because it is locked and padlocked. Now I go up or down simply to applaud, to prove to myself that I am no clod in these matters. It is the same with the carpet and the stair rods. I have studied them both with my eyes and with the tips of my fingers, in all lights, even the gloaming. I know where there are little blemishes, where the woof is going thin,

and I know the various stresses on the surface of the rods.
I have knelt. Providential that they didn't come in and
find me beating the ground with my head as if, like the
Arab, preparing myself to remove cataracts.

Often when I am out for my walk I get the distinct
impression that they are back, have let themselves in and
are disgusted at my habits, the little altar that I've made,
the candle grease in thick splodges on the embossed cloth,
various statues and icons, the shawl spread out over the
prayer chair. I don't mind what happens so long as I can
stay. I like to venture and make a bit of an expedition
but only with the certainty that I can get back in. I have
a spare key buried, in its own little clay hole. I am not
too sure of what I want to befall them, just so long as
they remain away indefinitely, for ever. They don't have
to die, just so long as they never come back. I know it's
futile but I still ask for it. They can become explorers,
heroes, huntsmen, lepers, anything, they can go native,
join a tribe. I am making a novena for that intention. Of
course I know it's futile. I know they will come back, and
maybe they will come before their time, surprise me.
They were hardly gone when a sheaf of flowers got de-
livered. It was a Monday. Winter flowers and shining
winter foliage. There were even camellias. I lingered over
the arrangements. At first like a Coose skivvy I stuffed
them all into a big ewer, and then I remembered that I
was master, mistress, abbess, and I got various jugs and
vases and bits of wire and bits of sponging and I made
the most ingenious arrangements and stood back and admired them and referred to someone as though there was
someone here to refer to. The last of them are downstairs
in the main room. Mimosa. They have faded, curled into
themselves and dried up. Now they have the audacity to
be falling about. Before they actually fall they are suspended in the air like buttons, soft cloth buttons of a
desiccated yellow. If I had a shrimp-net I could go down
and chase them but I don't. Even when I make a little

bounce and clap hands I invariably miss them. Bad co-ordination.

There is one little room that I am invariably to be found in. It has flowered wallpaper, the flowers neat as cymes, and it has a beautiful birdcage, turquoise and white. My niche. There is a circular table, glass topped, with postcards and souvenirs and leaves placed in under the glass. I am possessive about that room. I would like it to be mine. For instance I objected to the snapshots, the ones of Jonathan and Tig, as being too happy, too blasé. I removed them. I put them in a big blotter. Also in that room are gadgets that I play with. There are balls on the points of wires, and I play with them and tease them, and conk them together, and I make them fight with each other and make up with each other and spin round. There are four balls in all, attached to four different strands of wire, but supported on the same pedestal, connate at the base. They are different heights, and different shades, like growing children in a family. There is a yellow, a red, a navy blue and a green. They never tire of being pulled at, never refuse to co-operate, but then neither do I. The minute I go into the room I rush to them. They are on my list for stealing, that is if I have any prior warning of their return. There is a third thing that I covet, apart from the balls and the little table and it is a lady, a papiermâché lady, very gruesome but nice. She has big bubs, that even extend and grow out to the side of her and her hair as well as her face is streaming and green-black. I carry her round. She sits with me. At mealtimes I prop her up. She is called Instant Humility. Aren't names funny. I am called Mary. The luck of God I wasn't called Babette or Dymphna. No, I'm called Mary. At least they did that with a certain propriety. Plain Mary Hooligan.

The flowers were sent from the shop opposite the bus terminus, with a sign which says, 'Make friends, give flowers, wreaths and crosses'. Life is full of its little signs, little edicts, its little allurements. Yesterday on my afternoon walk I saw a most affectionate thing, a handwritten sign – 'Lost, black and white nursing mother cat, kittens desperate.' Heartrending. Dry mouths, dry tongues, dry throats. I scolded myself, I said to myself if only I could jump into a situation like that, espouse it as they say. I didn't. I don't. I draw back, perpetually, except for the odd foray of lust or agitation.

The morning she left she pointed to a trickle of whisky in a bottle and said 'You might like to indulge on your first evening alone.' I like my biddy any time. It is pleasant to lie on one's bed, or some swain's bed, with the alcohol coursing through one's veins, thoughts running amok, the brain like an old branch, or old vertebrae, seasoning the bitter reds of life. I didn't comment on her miserliness. I asked if she'd remembered her citronella. Coose palaver arses me. Then I referred to their picture window. We both stood gazing out, at a hemisphere that was sodden and grey as it happened. There was a bit of snow on the window since Christmas time, artificial snow sprayed on in the manner of flakes. The design was originally meant to have the contours of an anchor but time and chance and maybe even little fingers had tinkered with it and to my eyes it had the perspective of a cross. Can you beat that. At least it was a white cross and not a red corpuscled affair like the crosses of Coose. Right butchers they were, those graphic artists, everything red – togas, garments, wounds, sores, loincloths, handkerchiefs, towels, drapery, not forgetting the blood itself, the gallons of it. I refused to have the cross removed when the window cleaner came. On Tig's instructions windows have to get cleaned every three weeks. She does not like the grime to lodge, has some idea it will scratch the glass, maybe a well-founded idea, maybe. The master window cleaner is blind in one eye, his left eye, so as often as not the jut of his ladder seems to be aiming right through the glass, and as for ornaments, the lorgnettes and ingots and tear bottles, they skeeter to the floor at his very touch. I said to leave the cross. I thought it would assist me in litanising. The junior window cleaner winked at me and asked if he could leave his ladders. Nothing but ladders, to the ceiling, to the sky, to the denizens above and below. I hedged. I had a confrontation. I asked him when he would be likely to collect it. For me that is heroic, to pose a bald question. He mentioned an hour on the following day that was unduly early. I knew that I would be here in my bed, curled up foetus-wise between my hessian sheets, their hessian sheets, committing manslaughter in my dreams, or copulating with the succubi, being kissed by a whisker. No go. I shook my head. He smirked, then there followed an involuntary wink and he indicated the upstairs quarters with a tilt of the head. 'Apples and pears,' he said, meaning would we mount. I went right off him. The old quim went quite dead, dry as his piece of brown chamois. I had a brainwave that there ought to be such a thing as a quim diviner, just as in the Barony of Coose there were water diviners. Right mohawks they were, nearly always afflicted, blind or maimed, always pock-marked, marauding around the fields with rods and wands, giving false hopes, true hopes, no hopes at all. Ferocious appetites. Loved victuals, ate heartily, then ate the scraps, the giblets, the gristles and the adipises. Bad for their stomachums. Sucked upon the bones. Kept the little bones as dice for lot casting, a sport which they were demons at. Omniferous readers, if they are to be believed, read the fireside serials, about Brendan the navigator and the mighty Decannans and the pookas and the supernatural feats involving a Queen and a Dun Cow.

Little does my mistress know. I have wrought innumerable stains and I am champion at spilling. Also I scratched the hinges of the escritoire with my thumb nail. I did it absentmindedly one afternoon or one evening when I was idler or gamier than usual. I must have been distracted, maybe looking out at the street sweepers, an elfin bunch, or maybe at the shredded bark of the plane trees. I am still in grave doubt as to whether those shavings when boiled in vinegar are beneficial for diarrhoea. Not that I have any complaint, I am A1. I might have been looking at the shadows, discoursing, they're a terror altogether, intruders, coming and going, making Vs, breaking Vs, splitting and multiplying and contracting and expanding, getting unfortunate people into a daze. Not me, I juggle with them. I try to get them to do things, to make them crash, to make them stay. Oh shadows, don't go. Sometimes they desert me, then again they are so numerous they are all over the place, and when I kneel down I can reach them almost as they travel over the wainscotting and up the wall.

I omitted to draw the curtains during one of my debauches, so that the neighbours might have seen in. They still smile at me though, a grin. They are Korean. Maybe they are playboys too. High wooden fences divide us, black wood, creosoted; we are all aware of each other though, within our bastions, digesting, decaying away.

I've had thieves, a pair. I met the male half when I went down to the general post office. I go down twice a week in case there are letters from the lad. Sometimes he writes two or three in a burst, then nothing for weeks. It depends on where he is. Always bright stamps, very colourful, like transfers almost. I go by bus. It is very hectic in the centre. Different pace altogether, different genders of people, different mien, different skins; some loitering, some with a purpose, office girls wagging their wares, carrying cartons of tea on their heads as if they were Etruscans. I loiter, myself. It is more in the nature of a ritual. I think the longer I dilly-dally the greater will be the likelihood of a letter. So there I was, glued to a window, when this young man approached me. He was in the doorway and I was studying the poses. It was a striptease joint. His voice was very dry, unmelodious. He didn't catcall or anything like that, he just started to talk to me, about his mother. He had a big grudge about his native land, how they had to cross barbed wire and leave their jewels and their Bohemian glassware behind. He showed me a photo and I began to laugh because his mother was gross. She was sitting on a form opposite a harbour and it looked as if she might collapse there and then on the surface of the black and white photograph. The water itself was very still but she appeared to be wobbling, she being so rotund. Then he told me about the military academy he had been in, the tortures, perversions and so forth. I asked him to tea for the following Sunday. Had candlelight, a bottle of his native wine, muslin around the egg sandwiches, everything very *soignée*. I thought I'd be in privy with him but he arrived on a motor scooter with a girl. She was called Daphne, dimples. I concealed my disappointment by fopping around and proposing tea and a glass of wine at the same moment. They ate like wolves. I set a booby trap for them; I went out of the room on some pretext then hurried back in. I could have killed her. There she was, conveying his hand under her skirts, having a preparatory go. I went scarlet. I decided that I would fling them together, be their broker, rise above their little cuffuffle. 'Ah, the lovers,' I said. As usual I was unrecognizable to myself, I nearly always am unless I'm doing something ordinary like planting a bulb and filling in the hole with a little trowel, or making a batter for pancakes. He produced his etchings, snap-shots, she swinging from the ceiling and he with a big sponge wedged between his thighs, whereon his yoke so languorously lay. She blushed. It was a very nice blush, most memorable, and it spread upwards from her neck and throat. It was paler on the neck for instance, the neck originally being a blanched white, but on the cheeks proper the blush was reinforced by a pink of hers that was permanently there, so that her cheeks were crimson. All these different patches of colour on her seemed to be moving, changing shape, changing definition. She was pretty, delectable. She was younger than I. He undid her bodice. Even her chest had a flush to it. The colours were seeping through like port wine through a litmus. I held her, fast.

'I knew you would,' he said, taking one of my hands and attaching itself to his that was already adhered to hers, and I squeezed and I squeezed upon it. I was curbing my jealousy. Her legs were tight, thighs sealed, her very modesty a summonizing more welcome than a welcome. We were in the stately room, what Tig calls the Casbah, and all was very breathless, her gasping, continually blushing, his snapping teeth and his capable tongue, the vapours from all of us so gentle, so pervasive like steam. One of my tasks was to undress her for him. She kept her chin down but had her eyes raised in order to look at us both, a beseeching spaniel's look. Her hair was ash blonde but down below, her topnotch was brown, a mouse brown. She gave little halting breaths, looking at him much more than at me. Then he got in the buff. He was scarred all over and that should have been a warning to me that he was from the underworld. Like a pythoness she was, with her nails and her teeth, a little pythoness pranking things up. The hank that he had on himself, it must have been from his military training. I got the feeling that he'd be just as happy having a game of snooker. All through the event, even when she started combing his hair and brushing it with her wire brush, he was asking me if I knew any rich people. Then we had a very heated discussion as to what constituted rich. He thought millions, I thought less. All the time she was saying to him, 'Come on Milos, come on.' I got the feeling that he was not above bezzling. Asking me if I knew any dowagers who lived alone, was willing to be a stud. I expect he was with a gang, she too, loyal to him as I know now, loyal, an accomplice. He was quite cursory with her. The other thing he was interested in was horses, said did I visit any-

where where there were stables and could I get him invited for week-ends. Now and then he would jog her like
she was a mare, called her shaggy and frigged her. She
had shaved her eyebrows completely and there was something very drastic about that, gave her a gorgon's look, a
feeling she was formerly a snake. Quite rough she was.
She went blue-black easily. I felt I had to do something,
so I picked up a few nubs of coal in my hand and put
them on the fire. The funny thing is they never spoke,
there was no Daphne, no Sweetheart, no My little poppet.
Everything about him was fawn and epicurean but he
was lacking in passion. Biding himself. He stuck the brass-
topped poker into her and though she was refusing, she
was at the same time whittling away to her pussy's de-
light. All of a sudden he hit her, made her sit up and eat
a cardamom seed. They had a supply in a plastic bag.
Then she cried, got the sniffles so that I had to bring
them together. She said he had put her to sleep once for
three days and that she never wanted to re-live that.
There were little miaows coming out of her, soft and
sussural and it was very harmless the whole occasion, with
me there like some sort of statue, my stockings rolled
down but otherwise clad. I thought I'd better do something so I made a sort of platform with the mirrored
cushions and drew them there, as to a hammock, making
their foreheads adhere, ordaining them to kiss by means
of the nostrils like Eskimos. I lay next to them and said
things to them to egg them on. I had to rack my brain,
remember my halcyon nights. I had only to gurgle, to
approve, to disapprove, to ask for a big finger or a big toe
for him to reach out and acknowledge me. I thought I
was making a hit with him. I had only to pinch her for
him to applaud and vice versa. And when at last, and
after much dally, in the full spall and frenzy of their
capitulation, it was I who was most gratified, and it was
my name they both uttered. Soon they were twain again.
We resumed our conversation, they cleared off the sand-

wiches and the cake. It was sugar and spice and all things nice. Presently he had to leave to take up his duties as a doorman. She lay on her stomach, warming herself by the fire, an offwhite fishnet shawl covering her hindparts. There we were, scarfed, together. She kissed me. She told me that her hair was dyed. She did it herself. She cried a little, said they had no privacy as he always had to have someone, a best friend or a worst friend or a gangster or most often a cripple. She said the gangsters were the softies, wanted marriage and kids. I said what about his big fat mamma and we fell about laughing and blowing our cheeks out and making our stomachs distend. It was all frolic, the fire flames leaping on the panelled door, her shawl, her bangles, then the toast we made, into which we pressed the strawberry jam that I had bought at a bazaar. I trained the lit candle on her face, on her chest, because by then the dark had descended. I pictured her wearing lynx, her hair blue-black, her eyebrows in an arch, a tiara on her head. Her smiles so young, so true, even her little smirks. I wanted to put diapers on her and gingham dresses and turn her into a little child again, give her back to herself. I must have been inebriated. I saw all her ages in her face, her very young ages, her sauciness, her very bitter expressions, the lines that had been added and the ones that would go on being added, and her various masks, lies, wisps, paper dreams, untruth. She said we would be friends for life, like sisters, and she came up with a glorious proposal. She was to open a little stall, a sort of bazaar and I could work with her, come in as partner. She listed the things we would stock, beads, chains, purses, bales of cloth, all from the Orient. She had contacts in Morocco. I helped her to dress, even held her boot while she got her balance and lunged her foot into it. I laced them for her, they came above the knees. I kissed her then on both knees. She said she would love a horse, a bugie-wugie. We made a plan for Wednesday.

'Fell was the frush,' as they say, when Troy fell. Robbed. Under my very nose. I opened my bag to make an entry in my diary, to give thanks to God and the galaxies for such an interlude, when lo and behold, missing, my brown wallet, the utilitarian one that Lil cut and thronged for me. Most of my month's salary in it. Buggered.

Two nights later I was sitting starkers, on a tea-chest, with seven people sketching me. They all had sheets of white paper and I was sad to envisage any mark, any trace of charcoal going on them. After the flight of the thieves I set out for the High Street, to scrutinize cards in windows, where I had already seen offers of jobs. I put some system into it. I studied all the cards on one side of the street first, then retraced my steps and studied all the ones in the opposite direction. It was there I saw about the missing black cat, the nursing mother; and various sofas for sale and people house-swapping and soliciting. Some of the windows were lit up and even had twirls of coloured paper that moved in a swirl, but one was in darkness altogether, inside a porch and I despaired of finding anything. Still I got the Ally Daly of a job – it said, 'Wanted, artist's model. Teutonic, modest rates, evenings'. I felt anything but teutonic when I pressed the luminous bell. A Coose numbskull. They had already foregathered, five women and three men with their various accoutrements and brushes. Dabblers except for the leader who said he was an academy man. Definitely a Prussian.

'Open up, Sunshine,' he said to me as soon as I got undressed and got on my perch. My perch was a tea-chest on which I had to sit lotus wise. Fecund in its prickles, surpassing even the old horsehair sofa – the discomfort of it. To lift the epidermis in one place was only to invite a bevy of nips in another. The Jesusing that I had to suppress. I still feel that there are numerous splinters in my arse and no Good Samaritan to weevil them out.

'Open up Sunshine.' I kept looking at my clothes over in the corner, a ridiculous heap with my scarf spread over them for seemliness' sake. Seemly! I was like a polyp without my robes and my decoys. He kicked me with his corduroy slipper. The owner of the studio winked, probably her way of saying 'poor you'. I'd hate to see her undressed as she was in a very commodious garment and still bloated. There were no refreshments, just some bottles on a tray to grig me. I came to the conclusion that the thieves were a brother and sister team. Incestuous thieves. A power of good knowing that did me. There were a couple of hours when I thought one or other of them would come back with restitution. I thought it would be he.

I was already thinking what I'd do with the remuneration go to the Drake café and have a feed and then sit in a corner, mulling. They know me there and call me a Mick.

I was subjected to very highfaluting drivel about spatial conception and contours, my contours. They seemed to omit the fact that I would overhear. I was afraid I'd either get collywobbles or sweat, and that my talcum powder would flake, even wriggle. It had lost its initial gardenia smell. My pubes were like an old furze, tangled. I amused myself with thoughts of the gorse flowers, the yellow vistas and then the gorse fires on St John's eve, the night we call Bonfire Night. I thought how the lad would laugh, condone. First time he saw me in a pair of clandestine arms, he paused, said 'Shall I compare thee to a summer's day'. It was Moriarty's arms. There was no knowing what sort of spectacle I presented, face blazing, muscles fibulating, skin white and the knees a deep purple from my sanctimonious days. I was longing for a swig from his whisky glass, what with the sweating and at the same time the shivers. Their voices were very hushed as if they were in chapel. They took ages over setting up their easels and appointing the light and getting the perspective. Their charcoal made different sounds, different impacts on the sheets of paper, some silken, some more like a squiggle, and there was I, avid to know how I was turning out but not able to preen or not able to smile in case of disturbing the pose. I knew I'd get cramp. A bunch of amateurs they were, judging by what they said, because alas, I never saw the finished effects, due to a rude interception. He stood behind a lady called Hester and started to taunt her. It seems she concentrated on the outer edges of me, my hip bone, my elbows, the boundaries.

'But last time you said the perimeter was sacrosanct,' she said.

'Perimeter my arse', he said. And then he told them to move in on me, to look at me, to inhale me, to smell me, to internalize.

'Value for money, Sunshine,' he said, giving my pelvic bone a bit of a jolt. The one called Joseph was peering into my nipple so that it must have been reflected in the pupil of his small eye. He knelt and crouched and did everything to mock me.

'Get that arse open, get those hams out,' the Prussian said to me. Suddenly I could smell senna and the brews that Lil used to give us on Saturday, to be cleansed within and without for the Sabbath day. I had no idea how I was behaving and I longed to open my flapjack to see my reflection in the mirror, but even my handbag had been removed from near me. The tea-chest would squeak as I moved from one haunch to the other. He stood beside each person and then let lash. Thelma's was not fit to line a birdcage with. But Victor's was heartening.

'You always improve when there's a bit of naked quim in the room,' the leader said. Victor broke his crayon, in protest. Then picking up the pieces he went on as before. I couldn't smoke either. I was like a switchboard gone mad, sending different signals to myself – open, close, shut, spraddle, dilate, contract, Lil, Mother of Jesus, Jesus, St Anthony of Padua, fallopian, haemorrhage, blossom, alone, forever, never, hold on, Holy Moses, King of the Jews. He bemoaned the fact that they weren't in possession of a Polaroid. Tasty was the word he used, then. 'Don't ye baw' at me,' I said, suddenly, whereupon he got very vindictive and the Michelangelos were all screaming and jittery, thinking it was going to turn into a brawl, because to my astonishment I rose up and kept on saying it, and added a volley of abuse such as that he had black teeth and scurf, which he had. The upshot was that I was bundled out of there with my clothes under my arm and not even a sous for my excruciating services. I proceeded to dress myself on their front lawn, where out he rushed with implement, and abuse, and there was I skeetering down the icy street naked, yelling 'Don't ye baw'at me,' and he shouting some terrible threats about reprisals and what he wouldn't do. In the bus shelter I met a woman who ventured to ask me if I had just been rogered. A very understanding woman who said that her best fling was in the war and if she is to be reincarnated she's like it in the trenches but not Asia because the mens' organs are lop-sided.

Birdshit on the window. Happened without my notice. Bloody negligence. I was looking down at myself, surveying the zones that are going to rack and ruin. The poor old corpus, the corpus collosum and ciliare and dentatum and spongiosum and urethrace and the devil knows what. The bones are supposed to give revelations but I haven't had any yet. Soon I will be eligible only to play gooseberry, to wait under lampposts or at crossroads, while some wench is experiencing the ends of fingers. Getting nearer and nearer to the Corpus Christi. Lovely to throw the shackles of it all off and head for the transmigration.

This bit of shit is the same colour as the light itself, chalk white. It is irregular, not a full circle, not even a stab at a circle, a whitish splash with inlays of grey. It will dry out. It will freeze over. Nothing is nearly so revolting when it dries out. I am examining it, but I am not going to touch it or trace its shape through the glass, or press my forehead or my dinky little nose upon it. There was a time when I would and did. I used, for perversity's sake, to slide my hand in under the dark swamp of a hen's bottom, while the eggs were being hatched, the thirteen eggs, the baker's dozen, with the speck of cockadoodle dandy in them. Not very exalting that. The poor clucking hens were delighted and misled, rose in their fine bustles and clucked with gratification, thinking that I was rescuing them, taking them from their sombre chambers, those hay boxes in which they were interned, or those round iron pots that just covered the girth of the nest. Ah yes, I perused the inglorious darkness. Now I incline upwards and my most constant companions are the birdies, singing and flying and bobbing and dancing and pirouetting, the enchanted birds and the everyday ones, sparrows, the robins and the town starlings. Of course it is nothing to what it will be in the spring and summer when I have the fountains on and the lovely brickets of water will be flowing out and the birds very bossy and loquacious, getting plenty of insects and slugs off the various plants, converging on the fountains, singing, uttering, shitting, dallying to their hearts' content. Bobbing on the bobbing branches and never in danger of falling. Even now at the slightest sound such as if I ring a little bell, or rap on the window, they fly away but are back in no time, knowing that it's only me up to one of my pranks. I am agog to know those birds that live continually in the higher air and are never seen at all until they fall down dead. That is something I may never see. The funny thing is though, that the most haunting bird I have ever seen was an unborn, never-to-be-born bird, two-dimensional, sketched in its own placenta, on a wood road that was soft and nobbled from acorns and the roots of various trees. That bird was more of a bird than any that I have encountered in the bushes, or in cages or walking along the ground as they were wont to in Coose, when amorousness prevailed and their pituitary glands were gurgling. I can safely say that I have observed birds, in the skies, wheeling and circumventing in the autumn going south, in the spring treetops nesting away, singing, grooming, pin-feathering, eating, squirting, copulating, pecking at snails; birds loving, birds vehement, birds busy, birds dead on motorways, birds as they dropped into the scrub at the bid of the huntsman's bullet, and let out their little spill of blood that so beautifully complemented the feathers which were on the oaken or russet side; birds cooked to a fine turn, birds roasting; in short, birds; yet none have left such an impression upon me as the one I saw on the roadside, two-dimensional, intact in its own placenta, fallen to its death before it actually became born. So near and yet so far.

The next landing post after Coose was Liverpool. It looked different to what I had expected. I had expected it to be cosmopolitan but it was black, even the birds were black, and the tram lines were old and rutted. I loved it. In the mornings I could hear the railway carriages shunting and still half asleep I used to think that I was just arriving, and walking up the platform wondering where I would look for digs. We were a happy lot, four lodgers, all peculiar mind you. There was a very shy girl and she was called the 'Maid', a lady called Moira who worked in a club and a man who believed he was going to be a Count. We knew he wasn't, but it began to grow on us too, his daydream, and we waited for his big legacy. His plan was that he was going to move to Northumberland and take a big house and show films on a projector on Sundays. We were to be invited for week-ends. Some days, he'd put on a canary waistcoat and go somewhere and come back and say he had seen policewoman, Colonel

Porter's daughter, parting her hairs. He used to act it for us. Thursdays he always drew the dole.

Moira was boss, telling us how to stand, what to do with our spines, how to use our wrists to advantage, making us walk around the room with a dictionary on the head. Her boyfriend was a wrestler but we never met him. He was in London. We all aspired towards London, even the Maid.

At Christmas, the wrestler sent a card with a snow tiger on it and Moria kissed it and kept saying how beautiful and how proud. It had no greeting, only his name, a pseudonym as it happened. He called himself Prince. That was a whale of a Christmas. We clubbed together for the eats, helped in the kitchen and had the television on all morning. There we were cracking nuts and telling lewd jokes and pouring whisky in our tea. Even the Maid came out of her shell. She worked in a drapery, in a glove department, and was able to tell us about the toffs and how stingy they were, wanting the prices left on, as if by mistake. She gave each of us gloves, and apologized pointing out that they were seconds. After extreme coaxing Moira did her act for us, got out her furs and her green shoes, and her green stockings, and got up on the table, and kicked her feet and said things like 'Mister', or 'Give us a fag', or 'Cha Cha' and curled her finger. The Count being the only male got the bulk of her smiles and her erotica. Then in a loud belting voice she sang Biddy the Whore. The goose was simmering away and every so often the landlady, Meg, would bruise it with a fork to get the fat out.

> I'll tell you the story of Biddy the whore,
> She lived in a hotel without any door ...

Meg told her little girl that a 'whore was a seamstress and the little girl kept fitting on everyone's new gloves, saying bye-bye and Adieu and then putting them back in their tissue paper. Down on the floor, she was imitating Moira's steps and strutting and wagging her bottom. Meg kissed us all and said we were her children, her little uns. There was no such thing as margarine that day and we all had clean serviettes, very starched ones. We were a little intoxicated because of the mixtures – whisky in the tea, porter and then a wine punch, for the dinner proper. There was no rowing, no grabbing of the gravy jug or the landlady ticking off the Count for the way he used the lavatory the night before.

'When a man comes in late at night, he is to pee on to the enamel quietly and not pull the chain'; that was a frequent edict.

But Christmas Day went not unclouded. Moira cried and said she should have been the country's ballerina, only she'd grown too tall and the little girl then put on unmatching ballet shoes and pirouetted around, refusing to eat. Her mother would put a choice bit to her mouth, but the little girl would only kiss it and run away. For no reason the Maid cried, and said it wasn't to be married or anything like that, but she would love to be in the maternity hospital, having a baby, her own, whereupon Moira ran to the mantelpiece and clutched the Christmas card and said it was the most beautiful snow-tiger, the most lone animal of all and that her man was lone too. It seems she had shown her weak side by crying the last time she had had sex with him. Meg jumped up, blessed herself and said there was to be no profanity in front of the children, and then the Count who was stotious and over-wrought by the various emotions, removed his canary waistcoat and declared 'I am not going to be a Count, I am going to be a lavatory attendant, and I am going to work my way up until I am chief lavatory attendant of the Northumbrian District Area.' We all laughed but he took huff and said did we not know the sacrifice he was making, by relinquishing being Count of China.

It was soon after that I met Dr Flaggler. He came through the shop and asked where the food hall was. I worked in stationery. Very aristocratic he seemed com-

pared with the Count or the Coose Romeos and I was
carried away with his airs and the interest he showed in
me. He brought me out from the City to show me the
mouth of the sea and to point to Llandudno. There was
big preparation the first night I was going out with him. 'I
hope you are not thinking of wearing those shoes,' Meg
said. They were new shoes, procured at the January sale,
red, with ankle straps. The Maid had done my hair with
the curling tongs and Moira had loaned a muff. Meg kept
asking about him, was he a gentleman and was he anyone
of 'note'. She was very avid to meet somebody influential
in the theatre to help her daughter's career. Her daughter
was about ten at the time and is now an usherette in the
local cinema.

After the Christmas dinner we stacked the dishes and
went straight into the front room, to pull crackers and to
lounge. Very soon the landlady and the Count fell asleep.
The Maid kept opening her locket, (a present) with her
thumb nail, and in the end she put a little bit of hair in
there, her own hair as she said, for the time being. The
little girl asked was a whore really a seamstress and we
said no, and Moira began teaching her the words of the
song, and they sang it under their breath. Poor Meg's face
was contorted in sleep as if she was expecting someone to
evict her. She'd lived in one house after another always
having to flit, out the back door with her orange boxes
and her holy pictures. She suddenly sat up and thought
she was back in her caravan days and then seeing all of us
she smiled and lay back again. In the evening we had
fried plum pudding and totted up with tremendous satisfaction the different concoctions that had gone into us
since morning.

More mortification. Another room, another window,
that I found myself standing by, looking out, not actually
looking, glazed. There was a garden underneath. A small

garden jammed with climbing things. The big wide leaves were like big tongues, bladed, going up the brick wall. For some reason I expected lizards. I like lizards, their dartingness, their stealth. He was right behind me, my pick-up and I could feel his urgency. In removing my coat he said 'Mmm'. It was a ponyskin, one of Tig's. I have managed to pick the lock of the wardrobe and am on the lookout for a crowbar to invade the cellars. After he had removed the coat he comes and places his hands under my armpits and feels the little forlorn muscles there. I thought how as a baby one must have minded, riled against being picked up under the arms, picked up, or held up to be winded, or shown to others, to be teased, or be made smile, or to go gougougou, pinched maybe, or scratched, or prevailed upon.

We met in the park. It was an easy coup because his dog, a red setter, jumped on me. He called him off and then we paused for a bit.

'I'd like to sleep with you,' I said, wiping the mud off my lapels. I had no idea about his status but when we got there I could see he was a bit of a nob. He was dressed in cashmere and the upholstery was leather. To tell you the truth I was a bit quaky. I lost my daring. There was a lot of machinery, tapes, purring softly, tapes moving slowly and various speakers and amplifiers. There was also a machine for polishing stones, whirring away. He gathers the stones on seashores on week-ends. His hand was sliding down the texture of my dress, her dress, satin as it happened, dark blue satin with pleats. I was dressed incongruously, I was asking for trouble. He drew the curtains and put the dog out. Needless to add the curtains met without a hitch. I sat on the chair exactly as he prescribed, and took off my shoes. Then I stood up. He put his hands on my bum, for me to sit upon. His hands like a shooting stick, or a walking stick, the kind that toffs use at the races as seating place. I heard horses galloping and had the bright idea that if we would turn on his huge television set we might be treated to a bit of sporting. Eyeing me, eyeing me. A rum place. The machines purring. I got the impression that everything was being recorded. I didn't care. We were strangers. He said the word over and over again. It was like a little ghost in the room. There were so many chairs, episcopal chairs as in a cathedral or a great hall, as if each one was reserved for a dignitary. He said Close your eyes. He led me backwards. He knew which chair. He proceeded to remove my clothes from me, they came away without a hitch. I did nothing in the way of desisting. He said it was the only time it would ever occur. He said we were bound to become friends and our friendship would strangle our desires. He said not so rigid, not so rigid. He said to play. Play where? I wished for an instrument – plectra and lyre. There was something very secretive about him, suave, an animal, but with a velvet pounce. He had booked a phone call for Munich at a certain hour and kept referring to his watch, with its six little alarming devices. He only removed trousers and underpants. On his instructions I kissed him. He was pearled. He towered above me. So far away, or perhaps it was I who was far away. It seemed impossible to get any nearer, to get friendly or bawdy or wicked or wild. It was all too sedate. The park would have been a better place even at the risk of scandalising one of the keepers. I could see everything, his pupils dilating. It was like having my eyes tested, his eyes as torches peering into mine. We knelt upon our respective haunches, we exchanged no words, he said 'Ready, steady, go.' He had to tremble, he induced his own trembling, then he had to break away from himself, like a horse, bolt, become lost, convulse, let his throat muscles wobble; he had to ordain everything that he was doing, commentate, address his old valve, say 'Now, now,' time it, and then drowning his laver in his own cries, I cried too and Christ, I heard the screams of unborn mites in those two friendless siggers.

Oh deary me, so many base things, No longer human, but like bits of meat, uncooked, flinching, and still betimes looking for some little balsam, a crumb, some gob-stopping tit. When he opened his eyes they were wary, animal's eyes in a lair. It had been disastrous. There was no forgetfulness in it or no spark.

'Look out,' he called sharply as I rose. Threads were hanging from me, the threads that were erstwhile his, in loops, suspended. There I stood at that moment foolish and gaunt but then I put both hands under it and walked, or rather hopped, to the exit, clowning so as to put some complexion on the amiss. Thought of the cows and their composure. He was afraid the maid would see me, the frau. He went to reconnoitre, then gave me the beck, the permit. He let the dog back in and stroked it and nuzzled it. I was covetous for that animal then, for its uncalculating affection.

His bathroom was filled with perfumes and lotions. There were beaded bottles which were purely ornamental, and there were six different plys of lavatory paper. I let go of my hanging jewel, then flushed it, so that like everything else it commenced on its rickety journey out to sea. I weighed the same on his scales as on Tig's. Nothing had altered. I hadn't played enough. I hadn't played at all, I'd simply participated the way he wanted. I needed practice. When I got back to fetch my clothing he asked where I would like to dress. I plumped for his bedroom. It was utterly dark except for a slice of light coming through at a point where the end of the black blind had got torn, ripped from its slat. His eiderdown was on the floor, in a heap, cremeled. He too must have perspired in the night as I so often did, do, here; I mound myself with clothes in order that I can rise up in agitation and throw them off and say Begone and Fie. It is hard to imagine that I won't always be here, that this night will join the others, be a blur of half-remembered itchings and scratchings, be a tableau.

I knew it was time for me to be getting on my Pegasus again but I went back to take my leave. He made a few civil inquiries about myself, my interests, my hobbies, my friends, my other lovers. He was quiet and most considerate about everything. I told him about the lad and he said perhaps one day they would meet. I said 'It was a cinch,' for some flap-doodle reason.

'I don't even rate you,' he said, and hurried to pick up his ivory telephone. Maybe Munich was on the line.

It was bright out in the street, that winter brightness that comes when there is no sun and the sky's being looks to be tempered with steel. I often think people can read faces if only they would bother, people could have read mine then, which was mostly one of stupefaction. I couldn't breathe. There was a great boulder in my chest that I wanted to blast, to smash, to dislodge, to reduce to gravel or smithereens. I wanted to be pounded by Lil's potato pounder, be a spud, ridded of all life's paraphernalia.

I thought I would go home and masturbate, that was what I would do, but it was early, it was so early, so early, so bright. The sales were on and there was fifty per cent off everything.

I wouldn't mind a visit from the Holy Ghost, the paraclete with his tongues of fire. I can't master languages, and for a very simple reason, too thick a tongue, the words curdle. That's why I haven't been to Baden Baden or the Hermitage.

The lad sleeps out in fields, sometimes under a mosque wall. He has no bed covers, not even a net. I expect it's scorching and there are times when he looks down at his own feet and finds them skinned or blistering. Jesus feet they used to call him in the public baths. I can chart it all, the way he graduated from fuzzy socks to knitted boots to buckskin boots, to plimsolls to wellington boots, to leather boots, to football boots and then back to the merest sandal when he was free to decide his own footwear. Minor epistles he used to write whenever I was out of his sight. 'You are a big nit.' 'Pam pam pipe.' 'Remember the plum jam.' 'I need paints.' Always in block letters. Daftness itself. I can tell the different years from the different style of the lettering. In the very beginning the letters were like numbers, they were bold and assertive. Then he wrote in capitals, then he developed his own style of handwriting which was spidery. 'Come to my tree house for a Punch and Judy show, entrance 1d.' Perfected a code, a semaphoric system, the hanging of rags and utensils from a tree. Once he douched me when I stepped under it and said, 'Aren't I the witty boy?' That was from the time we lived on the big estate, in one of their cottages. We had a commode that we didn't dare use, had it in case of dire emergency. In the nights we used to gab. He loved hearing about the thanes and knackers of Coose. Above all else he relished the yarn concerning a joxer who came upon us in the middle of the night, surprised us, Boss, Lil and I, his lorry revving and squelching in the mudded field, and Boss declaiming Who goes there, and Sarsfield is the word, and Sarsfield is the man, and clothes getting donned, a trespass through the kitchen that was already inhabited by a different spirit, the lantern pumped, then lit, even its flame shifty and enigmatic. It was inferred that the joxer was an emissary of the supernatural. His attire was earthly enough, baggy trousers, twine round the middle, his gansy mottled, full of miscellaneous-sized holes. He had come with the express intention of covering the hayshed with his miracle spray to protect it from the rude elements and he demanded a commission there and then in the form of five readies, and upon such a demand Boss told him to scutter off but he held his ground, saying Up the Republic, and he had to be beaten away with lantern and the jut of the broom and afterwards in lofty tones Lil was heard saying that she had a hunch he had been sent to squeeze the foot-and-mouth disease into the crops and Boss tut-tutting and saying, 'I bested him, I cut the ground from under him, I told him who's landlord around here,' although in fact he had quaked like the rest of us and insisted we congregate near him. And there he was, complimenting himself, and there she was, rambling on about dead beasts, the economic war, a sacked land, dead beasts gaping at us, the workhouse, and Boss saying the intruder could go up the river on a bicycle. All of a sudden there was a bout of recitation suggested by Boss, to exorcise the panic, a snatch of verse from the eviction days.

On the ninth of December, it being a fair day,
We boycotted Dick Studdard I'm sorry to say.
With sticks and with stones we wattled him away,
Three cheers for the boys of old Erin.

The lad loved that, used to bounce up and down in his bed to it. And no sooner having heard it but he would say Tell it again. He loved the swear words and details of the joxer's gansy and Boss letting on to be braver than he was. He even asked to see a photo of them, his grandparents. It is a muzzy photo where they are both leaning on a pier and are curiously allied to each other, an alliance brought about by perseverance.

We were in a two-roomed cottage, everything ramshackle, the fencing reinforced with bits of galvanise and old wardrobe doors. We kept pullets and a dog. The estate itself was owned by a health farm. I worked there. It was funny tending to all the fat people, hearing them talk about food as they got slapped and slathered around, talking about the coffee with the cream on it, in Vienna. Nyumyum, Nyumyum. When I got home there would be the notes. Sometimes he had the dog on the table with a headscarf or a bowler hat on her. Laughing they used to be. The dog was called Rosie, a mongrel. Outside the window there was a commune of birds, about a hundred, and they used to grub in the fields, wander in and out between the cows' legs and then all of a sudden they'd fly, and because of their underwings being white and their actual bodies silver, they were like a whole lot of razor blades, darting up into the sky, cleaving the skin of the air. I got cream for free from the health farm and we used to have it with the porridge, or the pancakes, or, in season, with fresh raspberries or fresh loganberries from their walled garden. Some people don't know when they're flying it. I knew it then. Everything had a rhythm to it, my cycling in the morning to the crèche with him, then coming back to find him already there, having been brought home in the school bus. He had only to walk up a lane. 'Me a latchkey kid,' he used to say. He was very quick at slang. There was one note of his that I didn't care for though. It wasn't addressed to me personally, it wasn't addressed to me at all. I found it the day after he went to boarding school. That was much later and we were in a city by then. I had a job in Hull as a cosmetic manager. It said:

> Sometimes I feel sad for me.
> Sometimes I feel sad for you.
> Sometimes I feel just sad.

I crinkled it, bunched it up, not wanting to admit that he was prone to such thoughts, that he too had the pall, a bit of the Coose moroseness. He'd gone a long way from the dozy dazy times when he looked up at leaves and buses and played with beads and yodelled from the safety of his cot. All the joyrides he used to have. And laughs, nearly always followed by splutters. Made theatres out of match-boxes. He used to get in under the big brown table to fiddle with the castors. As the evenings got colder he used to reach up and pull down the green baize cloth, and cowl it round himself and wear it like a kind of igloo. Of course it wasn't roses all the way. He had a bowel problem. His father, Dr Flaggler, recommended a cereal, a special brand of corn buds. Dr Flaggler was very imperious, always faggoting his notions upon us. He said if the cereal did not work it would have to be clysters. We were in mortal fear of these clysters whatever they were. The lad had a rebellious streak too, probably brought on by his adstrictions. He scratched the paint off a newly painted lavatory seat and left the shards – they were a shade of duck-egg blue – strewn all over the green rubber mat. He got his come-uppance. Dr Flaggler produced the water bag, and after insertion and later the movement, the lad was dispatched to his bedroom and locked in without benefit of bread or water. He says it is then he wished he had mastered the Chinese language, because it would have given him something to think about, as his mind was clamouring for new thoughts, theorems, puzzles. No doubt he knew all there was to know about the boxed house, the drab garden, Dr Flaggler and I. So many little memories of him loom up, his constipation, hence his shadows, his cheeks like discs, the striations on his forehead, the pre-lines, mere tracings, presaging where the real lines would later be. They have begun now. He must have always bathed in cold climes because I have a memory of drying him brusquely with old towels and his skin mauve and his little teeth chattering together. He had a dream once of being one of the three Wise Men, on a moped and calling at a gate lodge to look for the infant child. That must have origined while we were in the cottage, since there were various other little lodges scattered around. At the same time I dreamt that he was on his tricycle in Times Square, getting squashed in by convertibles and trucks. He kept busy. I used to bend over him, brush against him, while he was drawing horses and chariots. There was always a bit of jam lodged somewhere

on his lips so that the kisses had a fruitiness and brought
to mind the orchards of Coose where he hailed from, but
scarcely knew. He had a little chain around his neck and a
St Christopher medal that he bit. Blackened his front
teeth. When he crammed pebbles up his nose Dr Flaggler
had a brainwave. He poked at the nostrils, first with an
orange stick and then with a wire. The wire happened to
be a clothes hanger that he snapped in two. It bored me
most painfully that usurping wire. No go. The pebbles
refused to budge. Dr Flaggler let out a yippee and moved
to the garden where the peony roses were in full rampant
bloom; the lad loved these flowers, their colour, their
chromes, their creaminess, the smell, their softness perhaps. In fact he had the bad habit of breaking them off
their stems and tossing them around as if they were toy
boats or one of his paper kites. Naturally he got whacked
for such usurpations. Consider his surprise then at being
handed one with glee, a full-blown peony rose of the pink
variety as it happened. 'Nice nice flower,' Dr Flaggler
said, as a tease. The lad laughed. He brought it to his
nostrils because he was told to and just as flesh touched
flower the realization occurred. He sneezed like an old
grandfather. The pebbles came cascading down. His
father had put snuff in the rose. A snuff and pepper
mixture. Ingenuity. He says his prime memory is not
that, but of a cow's tail and his hand in someone's, an old
man's, or an old woman's, a relation perhaps, a forebear.
Anyhow it was a white hand with brown nicotine stains.
It was after that he drew the chariot. Then he got out of
bed one night and descended the steep stairs by means of
his bottom, hopping and flopping from one step to the
next. He avoided the last step altogether and darted
cumbersomely across the hallway into a dark room. He
was afraid of being found. Still, he must have mewled or
puked or let out some little exclamation because Dr Flaggler found him there and surprisingly enough offered him
poached egg. We tried for other children. I was pregnant

on two occasions but lost them due to fucking. I believe our covetousness drives our future children out of us.

The day he was going to boarding school, we had to metal ourselves. We went by train. It was autumn. We came upon a little pile of sticks, then water with green scum on it and belts of young trees, young poplars, shivering, then more woods and tail-ends of woods, and jumping posts and horses and a bonfire and a solitary clump of Michaelmas daisies on a grass bank near a signal-box. I can see them still – insignificant and purple, a mournful purple at that. It is a strange thing that they did not remind me of field daisies at all, it must be the colour, it must be the difference between what white does to our sensibilities and what purple does. It would be nice to understand a colour, or get flooded by it, by the lineaments. Then came a different kind of wood, where the trees were very low, scutty, as if they had sunk into the ground, into mire maybe. Sunken trees, their tops bushy, like hammocks on which one could lie, a nesting wood as opposed to a forest where knights could fight a battle. It would have been perfect except for the situation, but come to think of it, it might not have hit us, the view might not have impinged were we on an ordinary day's outing. He said little. He would look at his belongings from time to time or he would touch them or he would put his fingers through the holes of his tennis racquet, wedge them through. The low farmhouses were so right, so friendly, so safe and even then I said to myself what am I missing, and why do stone walls and white gates and sheepdogs and blond roofs speak so, along with little bushes and the clotheslines and the garments going swirl swirl and all the other inconspicuous things and the white birds, the gulls, and the black birds, the crows, and the black-and-the-white birds, the magpies. We waited till we saw four magpies and recited together as of yore, 'One for sorrow, two for joy, three for a wedding, and four to die.' It wasn't the jolliest thing to say as the train carted us along. I almost said a daft thing, one of those heady things that gets said on state occasions. I almost said that I wanted to shield him against all awful things, against the reeks of darkness and the perfidy of people. It is the grace of God that I did not. We took a hire car and the driver had the funniest accent, an accent new to us, as if a pot of syrup had been spilt in his mouth. He said, 'There be gold in our hills, there be gold in Wales, there be gold in Hampshire.' Hills, dun, their harvest just stripped from them, the edifices of souring silage a decent distance away from each farmhouse. Anyhow as I drove off, instead of waving as he might have done, the lad did a side hop in the opposite direction, as if he were playing with ball or skittle. Maybe he was. Two other boys, no doubt newcomers, mohawks, were coming towards him and maybe they kicked a ball in his direction. Anyhow it was not the farewell that we feared, it was inconsequential, him running away like that, his hair spilling over one side of his face, and the object whatever it was, maybe a piece of newspaper, the butt of his attention. The first letter said, 'I eat the bit of cake with the cherry in it and think of Mamma.' He must have had the corners knocked off him soon after, because his vernacular changed. The letters got very perky and there were the nicknames, Tin Breasts, Huge Penis, Farnham Pervert, Gravy, and so forth. The food was called Muck and the girls, drips. The letters were very succinct.

'My aeroplane was broken so now I keep it locked in the modelling room.'
'I am making a yacht, circa 1900.'
'I don't know how to waltz.'
'I belong to the thirty per cent of the human race that has a bent spine.'
'I am making a table. Make no mistake, one table is not like another. Instead of quite thick legs, it has got thin legs and hidden dovetailing.'

'Did you know that when a branch comes out of a tree you get a knot. If same, i.e. branch, falls out, you get a hole. You can heal it with pitch.'

His handshakes grew more tepid the manlier he became, he knew the inference of such things, he knows the havoc of binds.

He writes now about the latrine service and the fruits that they eat and the mangoes that they stole, how perfumed and juicy they were. He has discovered all the uses for the mango tree, as a dye, and for pectoral complaints and as a laxative and to clean teeth. He is determined to get back to nature cures. He will be a healer yet. He did not use the word orchard so I get the impression that the fruits there are growing in the fields, just like the noble spud and the not-so-noble mangold in Coose. There are four of them, they gave blood in Morocco because blood is pricey there. He describes the tracks, the adobe huts, the interiors, the cooking utensils used in different parts. He seems very interested in what is underneath the earth, not for death's sake but for antiquity. Always off at a tangent – 'I have been to extraordinary places and walked over desert, and explored caves that monks lived in during the fifth century, caves carved out of cliffs, that are sheer, dizzying, in their drop to the sea. Sun, glaring sun. And I have been to the tombs of Abraham and Isaac. The landscape was fantastic, a movement of giant swellings, eruptions, corrosions of land where the earth has been stripped away, leaving rock vertebrae that look like monsters. The rituals at the Wailing Wall are too much, you should witness these. What a contrast of explosive nature between what occurs on the surface of this land and what the archaeologists find right under it. More, much more, but not now.'

It was he who sent the casket, silver with little mauve studs on it.

Going, going, gone. Like the walls and the crows and the ruins and the flat stones and the mere stones and the stubble and the voices and the kines of Coose. The perennial divide. First chiselling, then scraping, then the terrifying emptying of all but a sob. I don't mind too much. I mind awfully. I claw, at nothing, at naught.

Dr Flaggler, one of the original princes of darkness. Had a peculiar humour. He put a notice in the lavatory, having mounted and framed it, requesting that faeces only to be put in the bowl. It was a very old bowl, cracked, and veiny, like one of Lil's plum pudding bowls that eventually had to be relegated to the dogs. Once upon a time there seemed to have been a design upon it, maybe a spray or a cherub. The sign must have been meant for me as he didn't open his house or his gardens to any others, to the riff-raff as he would say. He was a curator by profession. It was an old house not far from the moors. I am surprised that I did not get broken veins, always out on the moors, we were, back and forth, walking and stalking; the wind impeding us, the wind battering us. We used to bring scones and a flask of tea. He was very pernickety about his afternoon tea. We used to sit, or rather flop on to some piece of heather, to eat and drink. The view was unvarying, endless vistas of heather, the sky itself reflecting whatever colour the heather happened to be, light mauve, or dark, or a springing green; sometimes a smearing black after it had got charred from accidental fires. In its green phase it stirred and was a bit like a sea, or sea spinach. I used to wait for the waves that never came. He fetched a rug one day, announcing that we would make love but I think too much preparatory work went into it, it was a sad ballocks. Out there you wouldn't hear a bird at all, only the grounders, the pheasants and tame partridges and moorhens. We used to try to catch them with our hands, very often we almost did. They let out a kind of cackle that was in no way like that of hens. More lunatic by far. The ferns used to stay from one year to the next, so that the young fronds used to rise out of the old, rusted, swordy stumps.

The sign in his lavatory was accompanied by a snow-scape, which is why I refer to his humour, astounding if you will. Ours was not a blessed union. Full of foreboding even at its best. For one who loved the moors and the misted fells he had an unexpected liking for babies, used to say he would rather kiss babies' skins than the skins of women.

It more or less ended in a little café on a bank holiday morning. The lad was three or four by then, and at home in the charge of a skivvy. The café I remember distinctly, what with its bright blue plastic chairs, all stacked up, its washed plastic tables, and such a wretchedly small clientele, and still the hoping and still the fluttering, like being in a banqueting place. We were on a bus holiday, a single-decker bus with amber-tinted windows. Five countries we toured and for a ridiculously low sum. I said to myself, 'It will be all right, this Erebus will pass, Dr Flaggler will mellow again.'

At intervals we – the thirty occupants – tumbled out into some city where there were bells and inns and a church spire. It may have been Bruges, or then again it may have been Brussels. Bells and stone façades do not differ that radically from one strange town to the next. We had to go through the side entrances of these cafés for our meals, and the foodstuffs put before us were unfamiliar. There was a man called Fred who was very chary about it all and kept dreading the prospect of octopuses. He suspected the dyes in them. He had been on a former bus holiday and was subjected to them three times a week. Dr Flaggler pointed out that that would have been in the south, whereupon Fred said everything being frozen, octopuses were as likely as not being sent all over the continent to physic people. He also testified that the

Danube was not blue. He had seen it with his own be-spectacled eyes. His eyes were small as nibs. His sister Ethel, for whose holiday he was paying, fell sick along the floor of the bus, and a glut of these foreign nutriments dropped out as she ran from the back seat, her appointed seat, to get to the front door, ran in vain. The rilings and the scoldings that he gave her! Reiterating that she should not have had those *crème de menthe* frappes and that she should have stayed away from Vienna schnitzel, since it was cooked in oil. His grey complexion was re-placed by another colour altogether, a scalding red. It was anything but becoming. I thought his poor nose would explode so vehement did it become. Everyone heard him except her, afflicted as she was with industrial deafness. She had confided that to me although it was apparent. The passengers did their noticeable best not to whiff or burp but what with the heat and the enclosure, it was not easy. Heads sought the window, Fred went on with his rhetoric and then somewhere along the way the courier stopped and broke off some palm branches which he strewed along the floor. It was then we smiled, he and I. A young courier, very smarmy. I helped him in so far as I trod on the palms that were near to me, to make better their carpeting. Looking down at the floor of the bus and seeing it green and seeing it rustle was like being plunged into a forest for a moment, and knowing that decay lurked underneath, that there was something rot-ting and decomposing, as there always is, even with Mother Nature. Dr Flaggler and I did not confer. He was the only male who commanded the window seat. Not that I objected. We sat, he and I, like two solid sub-stances waiting to burn one another up, we never talked, we never nudged, we were very nearly numb, yet we per-spired, we stared, we let out involuntary sounds that could be called abortive coughs or abortive cries. In the fields women worked. The courier would point to them as being a sight to see. Sometimes a woman would lift her head and a face would become visible under the straw hat, but the features were not to be seen so that it was like looking at rows of clocks that were unable to tell the time. They all wore kerchiefs under their hats and their skirts were dirndl and petrel blue. We drove all day and hence we sweltered. The windscreen used to be smeared with dead insects. By the time we got to our destinations so fatigued were we that we plodded out of the bus. In one of our inns I heard the rats scrabble behind the wainscotting. I heard them all night and so assiduous were they that I expected them to succeed and press through. I expected a great congeal of them. I was envisaging my escape, the ledge that I would have to jump on to, the repercussions from them. I had heard tell of one that had adhered to a hand by reason of its teeth. It was presented to a youngster by his guide dog. It being dusk and his guide dog must have taken it to be an odd glove or some matted leaves. The youngster could not shake it off. It just clung, dug itself in, and every time the dog went fopping its tail stiffened, likewise its backbone and likewise its clench. The boy was afraid to shout in case he frightened his aggressor. Probably the rat was frightened too, not knowing what it had got itself attached to. There seemed to be no solution when of all things a gentleman farmer went by on horseback, jumped down, searched for a big stick and severed them by taking a swipe at the rat, causing it to dismember as it fell away. There had to be a second blow in the lumbar region to extinguish its life altogether. It became one of the marvels of Coose. The youngster excelled himself by describing the clench as being like that of a burr. It appeared in the local newspaper, and the schoolmaster gave him a jar of Virol as a reward for his command of the language. The rats of Belgium did not press through, and in the morning, after the continental breakfast, eaten out on the little landing, there was the usual queueing for the lavatory and the usual dissertations about the beds and the bolsters. While we were queueing, the sheets and the bolster cases were whipped from our beds as the two strapping maids prepared rooms for the next bus party.

I danced in the night with the courier, remembered the crooner, my first. We arranged to meet in the woods. I looked forward to it, certain that we would embrace. I would have embraced anything at the time, a sheaf or a pillar, and my hunger was such that my arms used to lollop out of their own accord, reach blindly for some unfortunate person to hold on to. Another thing that pleased me was the venue and the fact that I would never be able to revisit it, unlike graveyards or old homesteads or cowhouses or the like. But Dr Flaggler became sensible of it either through the normal channel of overhearing or else with the sixth sense that he was so boastful of. He locked us in the small wooden bedroom. It was so hot that the gum from the wood had blistered into hard notches of dark amber. Nothing flowed except our hatreds. He said, 'You are not going to escape me, not now, not ever, you are not going out of my sight, you poor zealous wretch, you cannot make a life for yourself without me, it is beyond you, it is unattainable.' I sat there in a taffeta dress, meek and couchant, and I thought there was nothing for it but to remain thus, silent, slavish, imitating the fixity of death. Why such enmity and when did it begin to fester?

There was a time when he chanced upon me picking medlars in a field, and we lay next to one another with the sack over our eyes to keep off the sun, and he said, 'You make very good children my dear, you make excellent children.' Down underneath the boozing and dancing got to such a pitch that I thought it had turned into a riot, and each time when a lavatory got flushed I thought that the whole world was aborting itself out of existence. I had to feign sleep.

In the morning, we were scheduled to go to a mountain top. It was odd the way the weather went cold up there and the whole atmosphere was misty and foreboding. Like a sepulchre. Whereas down at the terminus it was stifling and the ladies' mouths much too garish and the men's backs raw and inflamed from their daring braces. They were all middle-aged people and though they worked in the same factory and lived in the same town, they boasted to each other about their gardens and their Sunday joints. They were more chummy at night when they were tanked up with beers, and then in the morning everyone was a bit irascible. They didn't approve of Dr Flaggler because he had brought his own block salt.

The little funicular chugged up between the gorges and the flowering banks. Very small flowers, probably alpine, since we were scaling a bit of the Alps. The higher we got, the chillier it got, and people were rubbing their arms to keep themselves warm, to fend off their depression. It was as if beads of water were being sprinkled through the air, water instead of incense from a censer. Dr Flaggler had a most challenging bout of noseblowing. The courier passed around boiled sweets, to help us with our swallow. I declined. He glared at me. I had kept him waiting in the woods. He called me a whore in the French language. I have picked up one or two foreign words for bandying. The top of the mountain was a plateau and there was the chanting of a cold, piping wind. A very sad madrigal it was. Due to a fog the view was non-existent. We could scarcely distinguish one another. The voices were suddenly subsided and muffled as if people were talking from behind masks or their tombs. Why they brought us up unless it was to introduce us to a sharp change in the weather, to make up for the fact that the bedrooms were like ovens and there was nowhere to bathe in, not even a pond or an artificial lake. There was constant grumbling and some were preparing to sue when they got back to their own territory. The only surprise was a settlement of shops, various booths, where one could buy souvenirs or lemonade. The women rushed and grabbed things, such as flags or bone paper knives, questioned the prices, then dropped them, incensed. Dr Flaggler hovered. I was choosing a spotted scarf. He said, 'Of all the tasteless things you have ever bought, this takes the biscuit.' I wound it round my neck, made a double knot, followed by a nonsensical bow. For some reason I had to get rid of my spending money, which at any rate was nominal.

I had a brainwave. I was in a fog that was vast, a great marquee into which everything and everyone got absorbed. I thought how simple, how elementary, to ditch him up there, to vamoose. No knowing what lay beyond the stalls, the restaurant and the two concrete urinals. I decided to vanish. It was as if I was expected somewhere. Expected? What inhabited up there? No little Red Riding Hood, no ailing grandma, the bear, the hyena, the lone wolf. Not lone – mothers, fathers, insatiable cubs. Did they attack *en masse*, as a pack, where first? To be eaten alive, to witness it, to hear the self letting out a hideous pierce, a hideous inner 'don't' at each rent, each mouthful, each gollop. Blood seemed to start to glitter on the copse, to infiltrate the mist. Phantoms. Sometimes I stumbled. I would put my hand down through the mist, through the swirls, to test, but I never ventured too low in case I should disturb or alert something, even a fox dining on a crow. My feet told me that there was rock and low scrub, and each time as I saw the shoe going down, I let out another prayer, another daft invocation. At times I ran and then again I halted. I heard a bell, a wondrous tingalingaling, and knew that my companions, my very own party, were begging me to rejoin them. I changed direction and ran now regardless of scrub, fox or boulder. They were waiting for me all right, some more impatient than others. The courier going Tch tch tch. I was too out of breath to apologize.

'She enjoys her little absconds,' said Dr Flaggler and he

mocked at the wear and tear to my shins and my seer-sucker.

'You never thought it would end in a public conveyance,' he said.

'I never thought...' I said, flatly.

Though there were many more blighted days and nights to follow.

Soon it will be St Valentine's day. I might send a card to the 'Duke', a Love-in-a-mist, or a devil-in-a-bush, a Venus's hair, one of my locks, and adorn it with a snippet about bloomers. He'd like that. Priding himself on being a true wencher and a true trencher. Poor Duke. Called himself thus because his neighbour had a bigger estate, and gave sensational parties.

Met him in a café, he was wearing a cravat he was, that he kept knotting and unknotting. Allergic to all shellfish except the oyster. 'Call me Bert,' he said. He had a rare command of the French language, and every other word was 'tartalette' and 'les modes manières' and 'tournedos', and how things were in Boulogne. We were in the Drake café down the road, diving into a feed of fish and chips. He was slumming it. I'd seen him before, often. I go on Fridays, my official night out. Their waiter-cum-cashier acted as an intermediary, said, 'Guv would like you to have a jar.' All it needed was for my eyelids to be raised and my eyes to give out their baleful looks for matters to be expedited so that his cutlery and his plate were brought and plonked beside mine. The condiments I already had, and a bulbous container for tomato ketchup with a green fibrous nozzle, a likeness to the sprigs of a fresh tomato, God help us. Straight away he asked if I liked things pertaining to the belly. I replied Yes, thinking on how I liked a nice pummel, or a nice massage, or a hot water bottle, I even had a bit of a yen for a Black Mass, which, as I understood it, entailed semen on the belly, a great gout of demons' shampoo. Of course I replied demurely, I said, 'Within reason.' He said how he would introduce me to the metaphysic of food, particularly the oyster. Rhapsodized about the shell, its conk-conk, the numerous little fissures, the lustres, the tubbed cavity where the animal rested, the sea smell, the flesh soft as womankind and then he was on about the uvula and the juices sliding down and the epiglottis dropping away nicely at the base of the tonsil. He described how the spawn resembled mere pencil dust and that the number of ova from one female was variously estimated, that for example Baster calculated it at a hundred thousand, Leuwenhoech put it as high as ten million and that either way the demand still exceeded the supply. I thanked God I wasn't an oyster. He complained about the ridiculous schism between pleasure and nourishment among the Anglo-Saxons, and said we would go to Amsterdam when the tulips were out. He had brought his own wine, a gravelly mead as he said. It was a beautiful subtle green, same as the skins of the white grapes that Dr Flaggler cultivated and that we trod upon in our wine-making sprees. It was a recreation to me, the wine, the company, and all that epicurean guff. Next thing he was on about caprolites – the fossils of hyenas! Scattered he says, like big potatoes, along the shores of that renowned beauty spot Lyme Regis. I caught on, because there was something so unfailingly Cooselike about it, these lumpen and possibly malodorous deposits detracting from the respectableness of Lyme Regis. I might go there one day with my thermos and my ash plant, play a bit of hurley I might, with these phenomena. I had my long wool dress on but no stockings because of reduced circumstances. When he caught sight of my instep, a perished white, he said What pearly pleasures and salivated.

'Strapado ever in use?' he asked.

'Get on with you,' I said, resorting to Coose parlance, a very clever palliative when they get saucy and want to fumble straight away. He was all for drawing my dress up over my snowy thighs and asked if there were suspenders to snap at. He snapped with his patrician teeth. Suspenders! There was no hose to hitch them to. Yes, he admitted to being a sensualist and said that on his country estate he was breeding a new shade of rhododendron, dunging it day and night – all sorts of dungs – mules, horses, jennets, his prize herd. He intended calling it Sufi after one of his ex-wives. 'You must come,' he said, and added that aubergine was his favourite colour, his choice for sheets, towels and bathrobes. Once it had been fuchsia, the original fuchsia fulgens, the kind that invades the hedges of Coose, hangs like trinket, like bell, like bloodbell threatening to resound in the sizzle of August. His list of charities was formidable. In everything he competed with his neighbour, whose house he had to concede was of better proportions. A consignment of spastics came on a certain day, in June each year, when the gardens and the grounds were at their best. It seems he gives them presents, little odds and ends, mittens, smellies and so forth, but always nicely wrapped with coloured paper and ribbons instead of twine. The most uproarious thing of all is their bathing ritual – he insists they take baths in his running stream, stacked in they are, chairs and all, at the foot of his artificial waterfall, the waters splashing all over them. He said they were up to every kind of stunt, every kind of trick. I envisaged being there the following June, sponging their backs or scratching them with long loofahs. I assumed that they undressed for the occasion, got in their birthday suits. I didn't know that relations between us would get kyboshed, like so many others, like all the others. I wronged him. For some reason that I still cannot fathom he has a porridge pot in his bedroom. Maybe like me he is prey to a supernatural ravenousness at night and has to get up and have a few scoops of porridge, but in his circumstances there is bound to be a little cruet with salt and a jug of cream to hand. He said he came once on a cricket green and for no reason at all except that he was batting well and joking with his favourite first cousin, an underwater biologist. A light sleeper, he always rose with the village cock and was often reminded of the local squire who used to arrange cockfights before breakfast and then start in on a game of backgammon or go racing or ferreting. 'Sure you're not catching a chill?' he said, outlining the bone of my knee, pressing, as if his fingers were pincers or sugar tongs. But dissertating about the daffodils, if you please, how they would be two and a half weeks late this year because of the snow, the beastly snow. The heavy falls of it seem to be over but it still snows in dribs and drabs and after I waken from a slumber I often think it's petals on the flowerbeds, a few forlorn ones, but still the precursor of spring. The flowerbeds here are all heartshaped. Out on the common, in the untrammelled places there are still lodges of snow, yellow and turgid, waiting to be shovelled away, or to be rained upon, or to be melted by sun. The sun does appear, very low and imperious, a red-gold globe of it, for all to see in the late afternoon. The only bit of warmth there is, because everything else is spectral, the faces, winter faces in balaclavas and dark garb.

We started a courtship, the Duke and I, meeting for lunches, and in the afternoon going home for abominations in his parlour, tea out of a moustache mug, the blinds drawn, the light latticed, suspenders for his titillation, babble talk, him saying 'Mary, Mary, quite contrary' and 'Out of me way or I'll smack your arse.' A pair of debauchees, sans shame, sans expertise, comparing what the different flowers symbolized. 'I call her the red lily lo', or 'My carnation, my Maisie's fascination', and then him saying that it was all a bit muchkin, and me turning into the little Widow Fusby at whose gusset he tugged. Not out of the book of Ballymote that. He is foreign on his mother's side, Caucasian, which is why we had raspberry tea and vodka out of a little silver quoich.

A lot more nature to him than most people I've met, asking how was my anaemia, giving me little treats, pippins, and even one of his china finger-bowls because I admired the bossing. Now he has only eleven in the set. Oftener than not he got the chauffeur to take me home and as we approached here I used to duck down because I felt so incongruous in it. A Bentley is not my habitat, somehow I look better with a cart, drawing it by the thills. It was all proceeding very nicely, the elegant lunches, the little pinnies from his nanny's days that I donned, crystallized violets, the ritual, he would say, 'Close your eyes, open your mouth, and see what Uncle Bert will give you.' Simpleton but nice. Then it got banjaxed, at a supper party to which he brought me. Very lahdidah. All 'Darling, darling' and 'How could you be out of our lives for so long?' and 'Isn't it wonderful that nobody's ill and nobody's abroad.' A telegram from some Godchildren in the Isle of Man – 'We hope you enjoy the smoked salmon.' There was a chaise for the coats and a locked wardrobe for the fur coats. The hostess had little leaves in her hair, silver leaves, caught on the ends of grips. She had just received a beautiful collection of shells from Australia, multicoloured, with various stains on them, so that you could see that they had just been vacated by some creatures, see traces of the life that had been theirs. These stains overlapped and it would be hard to confine them to a colour, so intermingled were they. I wanted to pinch one and keep it as a talisman along with the crucifix I have, and the heart-shaped stone washed ashore by the North Sea.

He was very careful to introduce me to everyone and I could see the ladies sizing me up, wondering whether I toiled and spinned or was kept in some *pied-à-terre*. I was very groomed. One woman was wearing a fortune, third of a priceless necklace. The other two-thirds had been snipped off and given to each of her sisters. It had been made into a pretty carcanet with fake gems to fill up the remainder of the choker and it was impossible to tell which were real. She used it as a gambit for men to draw near and conjecture and have to touch her pale throat. Then she became haughty. People were commiserating with the hostess because her pet, her singing canary, had got chewed to death that day when her butler, Louis, had left the door of the cage open and the cat got in. There was going to be a funeral and burial in the garden. Just as she succumbed to tears she would embrace some new person and say, 'Isn't it wonderful that nobody's ill and nobody's abroad and everyone's here.' The butler was nicely and it was funny to see him pouring champagne, his strategy, waiting while it almost brimmed over, in order to pour more, comprehending the monstrous and petty greed of each imbiber, including me. I think he had my measure all right.

The tables were laid for four, circular tables with cloths of tulle and stout candles in black sconces. They were angled in all directions so that no matter where you looked you saw the flame veer, and then under each set of sconces was a pan for the drips, filled with some essence, so that immediately there was a rare smell, a smell of musk, or maybe civet. The plates were differently arabesqued and the Duke and I went around choosing our favourites. Sometimes he would make a pretence of putting one in his pocket. They were Chinese and even the white part was like the whites of babies' eyes, permeated with a light blue. When touched with a fork of his champagne whizzle, they made an eerie tinkle and the sound filtered into the other room where the talk was cretiny itself.

'No wonder my paediatrician looked at me aghast.'

'Edward won't have his rare.'

'You should see him, he looks like a "Special Branch" man ...'

One of the men I was placed next to made love to his mistress in a bath, in Kensington, one night in 1965. Subsequently she vanished and he heard that she married somebody in the Royal Navy. He said a bath was *the* place. I didn't challenge it. He kept saying, 'Don't forget this was in the sixties before things got permissive.' All of a sudden everyone was clapping, some gent, head of a sanitary company, had gone to sleep but everyone knew that the moment his fork fell on to his plate he would wake up. He was cat-napping, a thing he learnt in Korea during the war. His wife was congratulated as much as he. She was called Georgina. She was wearing a nylon stocking around her neck and took a little pill between the first and the second courses. The second course was smoked salmon stuffed with caviar.

It was impossible to relish the food because of the struggle with conversation and anyhow the plates were soon swept away to make way for the series of courses. Individual soufflés were passed around and everyone cheered. On one side of me was the bath fiend and on the other a very officious man. He kept on insisting upon how well everything was served, drew attention to the lilies, the crests on the cutlery, the goblets. Then in brimful tones he told me about an evening in Poland in somebody's flat, eating cold ham and dill pickle while the whole household wept. Then there was a dissertation about striptease in Hamburg, knickers or maybe it was knicker-bockers, and the feats of animals and men. Now and then the Duke, who was next to the hostess, would raise his chin and purse his lips at me. It did not go unnoticed.

I watched their mouths. I watched their tongues, like tentacles, I watched their jaws, I could visualize my own. I had no business being there. The other lady at the table was sharp-bosomed and evenly tanned and she kept aiming her cleavage at the men like she was holding a motto to them. She vied with me for their attention, and the way it was I didn't want to be intruded upon at all. I would have loved it if most of them scarpered and there were only a select few at different tables, the courses very

93

slowly presided over, everything ordained, music, and then upon the arrival of the desserts, the warm crêpes and the cold chantillies, some singer or some harper to come and transport us until dawn, until the extinguishment of all the candles, until we were carriaged home drowsy, but glad.

A Highlander asked me out on the balcony. Said he was suffering from his post-prandial lust. A young fellow, face a bit pitted, wearing his clan's kilt. He asked what I did. I said I was a lady of leisure which tickled his fancy. We were confronting a piece of very suggestive statuary which was artfully lit and to which he was drawing my attention. 'You're a wee baster,' he said, the oaf.

'Let's slip away to a night club,' he said.

'Now, now, me wee lecher, no lady snatching.' said the Duke, and they had a bit of friendly wrangling about the Highlander's seat to which he lured innocent girls and fed them bees-wax and haggis. The moment we were alone the Duke kissed me, and whispered in my ear about the Widow Fusby, my garters, my hourglass waist – a thing I do not have. He said everyone thought I was adorable, especially Helen, talked about my charisma.

Then very solemnly he took my hand and proposed to me. He said he wasn't getting any younger and that neither was I and why didn't we do the sensible thing and take the plunge. I froze. I'd never heard anything so incongruous, me and him.

'I couldn't,' I said.

'Now Mary, Mary, quite contrary,' he said, wagging a finger and he talked about my little flambeau and our ripping times together and our stunts. He who had been in the trenches and had seen cities sacked and seen pregnant women with bayonets put through them, and he couldn't be on his tod.

'No Bert,' I said. I foresaw it all, the aubergine linen, the compost heap, the June, the July roses, Bridge nights, having to dress up, in gowns, in jodhpurs, in tweeds, the merry protocol. A whole new itinerary of lies and foils. I shook my head.

'But soon you will be on the shelf,' he said. That nettled me.

'So will you,' I said.

'If it doesn't work out you can always take a lover, a peasant, a brute.'

'Is that what your other wives have to do?' I said, resenting the aspersions about peasants. The very same as if I'd clobbered or unmanned him. He shook at the gills.

'No fool like an old fool,' he said, and withdrew into the room where they were calling his name to discuss with him the requiem music for the canary.

Old Slyboots McCall came forward with the kilt to his face to drown some of his laughter. It seems the Duke was in no position to propose to me, having a wife in the country, a woman with a withered arm. And the other wives, the beautiful Tilly, and the horse-woman Sufi, were mere fragments, invented creatures. I wanted to go in and congratulate him, and tell him he was a man after my own heart, a fancifier. I kept postponing it until in the end I was sloshed and not able to do it at all. I was brought home by the man who had witnessed all those tears in Poland.

I have had a game of snowball. Very erratic it was but livening. I never swore so much. All those young nippers getting the better of me, pelting me. I have a group from the block of flats, who invite me to their houses. 'Come up for a glass of cider,' they say. One has a boa constrictor and she feeds it one live mouse per week. I said I wouldn't touch it for a hundred pounds, she said she would touch it for nothing and wore it bracelet fashion around her wrist. She'll end up in a funfair.

The first day I met them they were under trees, cowering. There was something secretive about them. I heard them before I saw them, I heard the twiglets snap. Then I saw their shoes, their knee socks, those little spindles that were their legs. Three girls, two with brown eyes and one with blue. They came forward, stooping, to greet me. They were inside the railings and I was outside. It is a little garden in the middle of the Common, a little private place, sequestered. How they smiled. They smiled with the eyes and the rest of their faces were quite still, nearly impassive, but the eyes were shining, and agog. They were baking, they said. They had acorns as food and kindling wood in a very ramshackle pile. They couldn't stop smiling. It was like laughter that they couldn't control. One of the brown-eyed children had little gold sleepers in her ears and was called Conchita. There was one bit of shrub in blossom, climbing over a wire arch. The flowers were tiny and yellow, little yellow clocks dotted at intervals on the green curving branch, and still I would have sworn I smelt lilac, bushes of it, as after rain, the smell of wet lilac drowning, permeating everything. I had just bought an eiderdown in a junk shop. It was patchwork and hung from the ceiling in such a way that squares of it were close to the ceiling and other squares dipped down like balloons. There was also a picture of St Teresa, with her June roses, but I could only afford the eiderdown.

I could have eaten their smiles. They didn't just stop and start, they kept it up as if there were torches inside them, torches that would not go out. They seemed to be drinking me. They pretended to light a fire. Then they knelt around that conflagration, putting acorns on, taking them off, pretending to be getting burnt, pretending to eat, playing mother and father and house. They invited me in but I couldn't, I had one of my dates, one of my liaisons.

In the morning there was a plait of leaves on the outside mat. They were all bound together to represent something. I don't know what. Some of the stems had been slit to thread other stems through them so that it was a weave, and when I lifted it up nothing fell, leaves merely sagged a little, the way the eiderdown had. They came back about noon and said did I want my car washed, knowing full well that I am a pedestrian. The moment they got inside this house they ran round as if it were grounds or a ruin and they were pulling out everything and in no time sliding down the banister, fiddling with the fire extinguishers to siphon them. One of them broke a sugar bowl and we put it together again, piece by piece, the very same as if it wasn't broken. I'm going to glue it. You can't imagine their lilts. They were mad for the sugar I had, the coffee sugar. I had to put crystals on their tongues and then they competed as to who could hold it longest in the mouth without melting or crunching it between the teeth. They come on Saturdays. Sometimes we go out, we tramp off, a safari, through the Common and, if you please, I am supposed to teach, take classes out in the freezing cold, tell them about the magic rites of plants and about herbs and pond life, and what gods and what goddesses had for their emblems. Times like that I am forgetful and laughing. Later on we will picnic, and have a summer school, a hedge school as they say. They are intending to mitch.

My next Romeo after Dr Flaggler was a Finn. Had the air of a chieftain. Turned fish eyes into fish bait, and the flesh itself into a luscious stew. Had ideals, wanted to introduce market gardening to those who lived in the Archipelago, wanted those lonely creatures to grow lettuces and fennel and strawberries. Very carnal. Always roscid and rosy for him. It is a wonder where the nectars of woman lurk at slack times, the mateless eras. No sleeping at all, only a doze before the fresh violations, and the Finn murmuring his sea shanties. He said the sea is not dark at all because he had gone down, there were flowers down there, a different breed, brain and branch coral, figures like dolomites, fauna golden and bewitching plus spitfires and xiphios and playing fish. Beautiful his attentions, his assaults. Jade gate, Jade gate, Jade gate. He had a bit of Chinese lore. But in everything else he was a Viking, a sailing man, a sea man, a dark winding eel. His favourite animal the boar. Liked it all ways, somersaults, a maiden's closed purse, the old podicum sursum, the romp, the wrangling brandlebuttock. Saw women and girls as related to water, sedges, pools, whirls, creatures that invited him in. He'd have gone with old Scylla across the Styx, he'd have gone anywhere then. He carried a little torch in the back of vehicles, to be able to have a close look at me at any moment, my lips, the brown of my eyes, my teeth. We were to motor all over the world, or rather be motored, and have blinds fitted to the windows so that at any moment we could couch down and with his hands that were capable as butter pats, he could smack me into any shape or crenellation. Malleable I was. In the quiet after, I used to snuggle down, hearing about the islands and the fishermen, the kind of boats they rowed, their take of herrings, the spirits they drank and the dragons and sea-serpents that they feared.

He had a blind wife. A pianist by profession, she practised for four hours each morning and by an open window, despite the weather. The day I met him he was carrying a wicker basket, full of fish, all black and teeny, all squirming, their little eyes like pinheads, the same shade of red as ladybirds, a bright coral. He plunged them into a big saucepan and there they were milling about but milling to no avail. We were on a houseboat, a party of people. There was someone taking photographs, so perhaps it exists somewhere, the likeness of that day, an early day in summer, a breeze, the rustle of the reeds, the Finn in a bath towel, like a Sultan, the brine on his arms, the black crustaceans of shellfish changing to red under the influence of boiling water, various flavours of spirit, and the gallant way he jumped in to rescue a man from drowning. The man was drunk and swore reams at him and said he had not wanted to be rescued. That was after he had received the kiss of life. 'Then jump again,' the Finn said, matter-of-factly. The drunk sat on the quayside flanked by his drunk friends. All together, they projected their invective upon the waters. Nine grey men upon the quay, nine shadows upon the waters. The rescued one put out his begging bowl which was his cloth cap. Not one of them was without a bottle and a knife.

The Finn followed me to the land where the King has piles. Gala days, carnival, kissing and joking and kipping between meals, the Finn expanding, more than one man, a clan of men, an Eisteddfod, one of the ancients, in things and finikins, surrounding the bones of the house, ambushing, words soft, blasphemous, loud, incantatory; balls sacheting, breeches down, buttons, cracked leather buttons rolling all over the floor, the Finn making grunting sounds, the execrations and then the little bits of slop, the same words as in an autograph book – love and violets and always and ever and now; the Finn drawing the drapes, donning a nightshift like Old King Cole, feeling the bedcovers, climbing, saying Heigh ho and the sea shanties. A kind of embargo, the billow, the bruises, the bites, tossed, and turned, inside out, raucous, dulcet, a pandemonium, rumps rearing, slathering, words, wet words, tongues, coals, baskets of fire, and devil's pokers going through.

And yet there were the intervals that had to be filled in, the gaps, the times when people say to themselves 'What am I doing here?' or 'What is my partner thinking?' He broke up boxes for kindling and whittled some into spindles. He stacked the logs. With his knife he sculped, made little manikins and mermaids and little boats and oars. He bought slices of steak, thin as parchment, dipped them in oil and cooked them on the open fire. He presented them to me on a long fork, the toasting fork, and watched while I chewed. The oil dripped all over the place, it was in little drops, in droplets, with a rainbow skin. The fresh fillings fell out of my teeth but I chewed and I smiled, the way happiness ordains it. Nearness, farness. How long more would he stay? Yet there was hope, voiced hopes, like beacons in the dark. He would bring me to the sea-girt isles, I would meet those men who fished and drank, see their galleons, listen to them lusting for women on their nights away, the one in particular who said that when he had a head-cold his handkerchief resembled a starfish. Women and starfish and the Baltic nights. I would stay there, copulate, be his gilly, his sea cow. He carved his initials on the table, the mete-board. We did not talk about his wife, except on one point. I asked if she was blind from birth. I still don't know. He said that in one of her dreams she turned him into Santa Claus and that he was dressed in a garish red. That gave me the impression that they were close, that they exchanged dreams in the morning when they first surfaced. In sleep he ground his teeth. He cried. He went to the travel bureau and confirmed his return booking.

There followed the letter – 'I am slowly finding out that I am in love with you.' A long silence. The time when love burrows. He and his wife went south to take the sun. I headed for there. Impetuous those days and also I had saved a bit of cash. One morning in the land of Spain, after a torrent, and with the earth still up-turned, and the terraces in a state of near collapse, I waited for him. It was a new hotel and they were plastering and doing last-minute things because it was due for inauguration within a week. The atmosphere was very hectic, with men pushing wheelbarrows, and men hammering and the scaffolding anything but sound, while outside, the gardeners with plastic cement sacks caped over their shoulders, were planting petunias for the great day. So sweeping were the pools of water that the petunias moved away as

on floats, not settling anywhere in particular, just ambling about in the water like crusts of balsa boats. There
was a conference of musicians and one who rolled his
pupils incessantly came to tell me that they had an earth-
shattering discovery, that Toscanini had the same wave-
length as Bach. He was telling everyone, even the
workers. I was afraid that his eyes would pop out of his
head. The taxi driver came back wearing leggings, which
means he popped in home on his way. I read a typed note
– 'My husband is away, he will be back perhaps next
week, perhaps not.' It was signed with her Christian
name, Tora. I wondered, who had read it out to her, who
had transcribed? I wanted ridiculously to send her back
something, a grain of sugar folded up in a tiny twirl of
paper. So that was that.

In the unfinished dining-room there were only four
guests, the waiter, two chess players and myself. I got
drunk on rum. That used to be his drink. The waiter
offered me the loan of a bath to sleep it off in, a sunken
marble. I slept with a towel over me, dreamt, dreamt of a
sea-shore with coloured canvas shoes laid out but adhering to a pattern that was both beautiful and eerie. I was
barefooted in the dream, like Lil in her schooldays.

When the time came to waken me the old waiter
splashed cold water all over my cheeks and smiled and
stuck out his tongue. He had changed into a jacket, green
velvet, neat little darns on it. I declined his kiss. He said I
could not blame him for trying, I said 'No blame, no
blame, no.' There ought to be crèches where poor people
can go when their glands ignite, just as there are wailing
walls, and temples to chant in. At home in the night,
there was an earthquake that came all the way from Gib-
raltar. It shook the foundations of the little villa that I'd
been loaned, and the walls wept and the plywood doors
swelled. I could not get out of the bedroom. I pulled,
pushed, shoved and eventually had to bolt through the
window. Up on the highway a lorry driver gave me a lift.

He was a very corpulent driver with a wheeze. I knew that the Finn was somewhere, behind some window or wall of a ghastly urbanization, reinstated in the arms of his blind wife. In the first lit-up town that we came to I jumped down and the lorry driver hooted at me for not having given him warning. At the airport I bought cultured pearls and soap in black crêpe-paper wrapping. It was a beautiful flight, ethereal up there, away from everything, the eddies of air, blue light, the clouds like down asking to be danced upon.

He wrote some time later.

Impossible to see you
now –   cannot leave
NEXT TIME
Always next time

Next time
next time
next time
    Next time
is now last time,

I post this to you directly.

I answered it in one fell swoop.

'I sit here hating you. If I have said I loved you, dismiss it. When one sees the bright postcard happiness one spits on it, the puny possible has always belonged to others as indeed it does to you now. You have a wife, blind, blonde, you say, I hate her. I would tear her limb from limb as does the dog the bunny rabbit, and eat her, and presently vomit her, so as not to give her the satisfaction of my digestive juices. You came from her to me. You cur. I professed to love you. It was all lies, junk. That is my slavery, my gift for untruth, histrionic, rather like inheriting moles or an aquiline nose. Forget it, Buster.'

I picked up that slang in New York, where I once went to promote Coose. That was in my prime. Very laughable. My task was to lure the unfortunate exiles back to the Old Bog Road, the trout streams and the potlatch ceremonies. Met a police chief who told me straight out he was a gun-nut. He had four revolvers in his pocket, a six-footer, whose wife didn't buggy whatever buggy is. They all said the same things – 'Kiss my ass' and 'Ohboy ohboyohboy' and 'Nope' and 'Gawd' and 'Poignant'. Most of the time I was plastered, from drinking new concoctions. Another nut with leaflets told me I wasn't fit to be a rucksack on Bessie Smith's ass. More ass. Neither was he. There were turkey sandwiches in all the delicatessens although it was nowhere near Christmas. I saw a sign in a lavatory which said, 'I came into the world crying and I've been crying ever since.' It was signed Emily. It was done with very yellow excreta, fresh and mealy. When I came back to my table and told my escort – an advertising mogul – you'd think I'd given him a garland. He brightened and proceeded to tell me that when his wife had cancer of the brain, and his lady-love had cancer of the body, only then, filled as they were with tubes and physic, bound for death, only then could he fuck them at all. I must have smiled because he said what a nice smile I had, what a nice little curling lip, and he invited me home so that he could take pictures, for his album. All his family had ended up in incinerators. I baulked. I could feel a spot of cancer creeping into me like mist or verdigris and I am no one for being bedridden.

I can hardly sustain myself till morning. I would have got up long ago only I have a feeling spirits invade rooms at night and if this were vacated they would invade it too. They shy from me fortunately, from my mortality. Maybe they fear me, see in me a plague.

Then the regaled mogul proffered the information that a lady of mixed ethnic origin whom he had met in Miami, told him 'It was no bigger than a pearl.' They were down by a pool. 'But,' said I nonchalantly, 'a pearl is a pearl is a pearl.' He went berserk, called me a crapper, a jerk, a mother-fucker, a cock-sucker, a souped-up bag. I fled and finding myself safely ensconced in a taxi, my bemusement was such that the driver who was Mexican and called José invited me to sit out front with him. Why not. I was flexing and unflexing my calves so that I would acquit myself well on the float the following day. I was scheduled to travel along the main avenue, doling out shamrocks and doing a bit of step dancing, inveigling, boggling them with Kiltartan drivel. I sat next to him. Pure greenhorn stuff. I thought it was a gas to be out there, head on his shoulder, him panting in old Mexican, the vehicle crazying about the streets and his name and his family name, plus his licence and a likeness of him staring back at us; his slingball as long as Lug of the Long Arms, ochre, reminiscent of the gladed mushroom, sprouting into fiendish and gigantic proportions. It could have steered the car and for a time it did. He began to lose sight of his obligations as a driver. People gaped in, brandished fists, wagged ferrules of umbrellas or maybe it was sunshades they were wagging. Vindictive people. Everyone there looked deprived, especially the people serving in the shops. 'Aw shucks,' he said back to them. It was Aw shucks, or more, more, mas. He was waxing. He suggested a hotel. I said better his lodgings. I was tipply and several thousand furloughs away from the jurisdiction of Coose. He said Baby, baby, baby. He said cinco minutos it would take. That staggered me. He was steaming. Rooms, rooms, rooms, he said, tearing off into a side street. I foresaw some joint, the signing of a book, a key, maybe two keys, a flight of stairs, sleaziness, a big bill and subsequent hassling. The tourist chief didn't give me a very flush expense account, and as for my hotel, it was a shebeen, with empty detergent packets on the windowsill, and the previous inhabitants' chewed sockets. So I grappled with him, there and then, and using his sirdar cap as a porous font, I issued a few fond words while a great animal leap, a glorious leum spurted from him, whereupon I shot from the taxi and ran for it to a photographer's studio where I was expected. The last thing I heard him say was 'No bueno, no good.' Talk about hyperbole. I was lucky I didn't get arrested. Needless to add I was in tatters and askew.

Lately, I'm thinking that if I'd kept some of these emissions instead of squandering them so, that if I'd put them in a little jar or a test tube, I could have done a bit of experimentation, dabbled in the mysteries of botany. No knowing what might have emerged, a plant, gestation, a half-thing, a creature, nearly with animation, on the borders between animal and plant, no feet, moving by means of its cilia, always moving in the daylight, in the dusk, in the dark, with something of the phosphorescence of the glow worm or the ocean, a little wandering infuseria. I could have given it names, mused over names, the way expectant parents do, consulted a book. I forsook all that, the domestic bliss, spurned it.

Still, I wouldn't have it any other way. The raptures make up for everything, even the doldrums. Like screens or roses just floating by, wondrous the colours that crop up in me, moving along like barges, nice, pink, with a lining, a thousand, thousand sundowns.

Then there are the faces, some I have met, some not, heroes if you please, genii, more mouths than could cram in Babel, faces from the east and the west, a flux, a flotsam, then the dancing, the beautiful precocious dancing, sheened limbs, persons only just grazing each other like the spruces that appear to brush the heavens in moonlight.

These must either be a foretaste or an aftertaste or else they're some little thing sent to keep me going. Oh sweet worrisome briar, oh sweet vertigo.

Not always placid either. Tight squeezes, very often on

the brink of suffocation I am, of a scream, the joys giving way to the shudders, a tempest, a terrible tempest. But it is beyond that I have to go, anyone has to go, for there to be satisfaction in it, for there to be the real pageant, for one to be conducted through the fire.

Very soon I will be accustomed to killing. As murderess, I list a mere three – Boss, Lil and Lightfoot; not the lad, more than likely he has the irons over me, beautiful little blackguard. He knows how to amputate.

I did take up arms not too long ago, the weapons were ludicrous, warm human flaps of flesh, in strips, brimming with blood, more like pies, and we all having a good go at one another, the enemy side, our side, identical weapons, milling, and pressing back and forth on the plains, the interminable plains; no cavalry, all infantry as far as I could tell. I didn't get the jitters or anything like that. Then God appeared, parting the heavens in his imperious way, a broth of a boy, hoarse-voiced in white of course, white broderie anglaise, telling all and sundry to quit such considerations, earthly feuds, to remember the writs, to get back to prayer and tillage. When I tell people they laugh but I laugh about their budgerigars.

I had quails' eggs yesterday. I bought six but ended up with five. They have a very particular yolk, nearly pink, fine tasting.

'Six quails' eggs,' I said, first in the queue.

'Huh – two herrings please,' said the woman behind and then proclaimed I was a glamour puss. The man serving me was irate. He pretended not to hear her. He put the quails' eggs in a papier mâché box, but since they were too big for the sockets, they were wobbling and he said they were in danger of breaking. He went away to get something and though I thought it would be chaff, it turned out to be wood shavings. There was an echo of the forest.

'Going to a funeral?' she said, addressing him, and then started to poke things with her cane, to comment on the quality of the skate.

'Offal,' she said, 'frozen offal.' He said there was no need to be so toffeenosed and I thought she would strike either one of us.

Then in the pub where I went to get a glass of wine, I had another peradventure. It was a slack time and there was a woman talking to a man, her voice very pleased with itself, saying how she had good taste, excellent taste, and that her three best chairs, her Chippendales, were beautifully scattered around her house – one in the hall, one in her bedroom, one in the lounge. I decided that her hearer was her lawful husband and that it was their one talking point. He looked vacant, his eyes were like the flecks of snow. Suddenly she said she wasn't going to sit in a saloon bar with a person of my ilk. I was somewhat flamboyant. I often paint my cheeks to give myself and others a little startle. Another time I might have looked quite ordinary in my brown astrakhan and without the caste mark on my forehead. There we were, two women refusing to budge. Like two odd bullocks thrown in together at a market. Her husband was trying to calm her down, assuage her, and in the end what she did was to put a handkerchief over her face, and secure it down with the brim of a fustian hat. Every time she took a sip a bit of handkerchief got in the way of her mouth. Once she was blindfolded he was making winks at me as if to convey what a shrew she was. He was no Casanova either. Then by a coincidence the woman from the fish queue came in and I thought there was going to be a positive onslaught. I made room for her. She ordered a gooseberry wine and said to get this, that she slept alone in her four foot six bed and her husband slept alone in his four foot six bed and no regrets on either side. He got up at two a.m. to let out the dog, but he would have to get up anyhow as he suffered with his kidneys. 'Nice,' she said, alluding to my wine. I showed her the eggs and their beautiful speckles. She held one to her ear and after a bit of coaxing had it in her sherry, raw. Such a good, such a true heart possessed her then as she sifted the bits of shell in the palm of her hand and glowed, like a kind of dumpling. 'I am earthy,' she said, 'but I dream sometimes.'

Still, little by little the circle dwindles. One has to admit that things are thinning out, handshakes getting more limp, birthdays getting forgotten or ignored, people dying or emigrating to Australia, people going bonkers, or taking umbrage for the remainder of their lives. Madge is a case in point. A big wall or a gangrene has risen up between us. We can't forgive. Or rather we can't comprehend the spite that possessed us. I won't see her again, not till her funeral probably. She might even outlive me, her mother lived to a ripe ninety-four. We shared a flat once, iced cakes together, and carded wool. She got me this job, sent the clipping that brought it to my attention.

'Sonofabitch,' she said, coming down with a mink over her shoulders. I arrived in the middle of the night, one of the occasions when I got the bejabies and thought that it might not stop at that, that Lil might come, with a sodality, her sisters in Christ. Madge was thrilled. I made straight for the fire and unraked it. She gave me the bellows. I had some notion that I'd kip down there for ever. That's what I craved, to stay with someone, to give this place the go-by, to have chats and unions in the evening. She produced cold roast pork and tinned apple sauce. There was snow and a blizzard. In fact it is a record night for snow, one in the annals, one when tramps must have cleaved to the ditches like hens do in rain, and in trepidation. Through the big window we could see it spinning, falling, and it was as if the night was turning into some kind of vast corpse that had to be watched and waked over. We were glad of our drop.

'Tell you what,' she said, 'you don't want to live but you've got to live, right?'

She knew that I'd come with some tale of woe, some conchology and she put her finger to her lips and said, 'You wanted to talk about something. Do me a favour. Don't.' She said the times was zero, all zero, but fun, good fun. She carved and while she was still carving I was picking, scrounging, eating the best bits of crackling. Her husband Buzz was not her husband proper, for the seventeen years prior to their divorce. She did everything to keep it together, gardened, bought a pressure cooker, learned how to shake cocktails, how to be a poker player and a pretty girl. From behind a platter she produced his letter. It said how rotten he treated her, how life had passed them by, how his new girl had stubbed a toe. The wine was from Italy and tasted of resin. I thought of sun and a holiday, rock faces and the little strands of hyssop, lilos getting blown up, children and dogs sploshing and jumping into water, lovers eating the same dish, maybe paella, so that they would have the same breath smell when they went up for a siesta. It was like being there. I didn't have to picture it much. 'Do you know who I hate?' I said, on the spur.

'Who, what?' she said, in a whisper.

'Loving couples,' I said.

'Innaresting,' she said.

She punched the dresser with glee. The crockery began to waver. It was a low Welsh dresser with jugs hanging from all the hooks, and they shook quietly long after the wood had subsided. In the field outside, a mare was being mounted by a stallion, black as serge.

'Look, fucking,' Madge said. His hooves girded her middle, his great mane rose in the air, and we waited, but all of a sudden the mare bucked as the stallion slipped and fell.

'Jesus Christ,' she said, thinking he had damaged a leg. She mentioned the year's losses which were preposterous and which she blamed on Bluett, the cowman. He had found her once when she'd taken an overdose and pumped her, used the stomach pump that he had for beasts. After a brief gallop the stallion cornered the mare again. We clapped. She was still as a stone mare and we thought, grudging.

'Yes, my old man, Buzz, he beat the shit out of me,' Madge said, and flung the letter into the fire. She riled against her maker, that all her buzzies were hapless, losers. Outside was very stark, the night, the bare field, the serge black flitches as they rose in the air, the mare so brown, so abject.

'Impotent bastard,' she said. The stallion had slipped again. She said Buzz wasn't even there for her two miscarriages, was cleaning up Europe after the war, making friends with German doggies, mountain doggies and so forth. She laughed and was snide, said everyone had a grubby fantasy when you got past the bullshit. More snow was falling and everything was getting fastened, her voice in my head, the mare and the stallion with nothing to graze or chew on, and not able to mesh. When she opened the window there was a slushing sound as the stallion trudged round and round clockwise in the boggling snow.

'Tell you a secret,' she said, winking.

'Wedding night, had to put bows in hair and do cancan. Threw things at me, said get off that stupid dressing-table.

'Sonofabitch, he was the one that asked me to get on in the first place.

'Tell you another secret,' she said, opening another bottle of wine. The cork crumbled and she had to force it in. She kept muttering, 'Boy, wait for it because it is going to be creamy.' It was a Greek wine and more acrid than the other. A little girl she was, thinks she hadn't menstruated, when she had to accompany her mother to a big store, to meet ladies for lunch, where she got cramps, then diarrhoea, had to decline the lunch, was teary, but going home in the bus, with the street lights already on, she saw a man in overalls, who looked at her, right into her, and she had a sexual experience, the jellying, a womb wave, her very first, the first big dip.

'I'm fine,' she said, 'just fine.' But she looked raddled.

'Know what I did?' she said.

'When he took up with that broad Jody I went to a hotel where they were spending their dirty week-end, brought Bluett who eats enough for four, so we treated ourselves to the best champagne, the best Beluga caviar and the very highest venison they had. When the check came I signed his name alongside his room number and I sent it up with a note on a Kleenex, "Super lunch darling," then I left.'

I shook my head and she shook hers, slowly, reproachfully.

'You don't want to live, but you've got to live,' she said, and poured the wine with a flourish. At that second we jumped. The stallion was on the mare, cleaved to her and though it was impossible we thought we'd heard the jissoms flow.

'So what do we do now, angel,' she said and gave me a big hug. The dregs she and I. The light was stark, searching. The dawn was brighter than any normal dawn, brighter than this. We stood there watching, enthralled, half drunk, in an embrace. I could see her predicament. I could touch it, it was like an opening in her chest, being let look in. Into her plight. Some part always remains inviolate, there dwells a skeleton within that nothing can blemish, that no feeling can tamper with. She was an inveterate then.

She ran and got bread and put it on the outside ledge of the window, and the birds came out of their hiding places and the gulls came in from their roosts above the sea. But there were no cawings and no songs. The snow numbed everything and time seemed to drip, tick-tock, tick-tock. As the bread froze she scooped it up, held it under the warm tap, kneaded it, and played. It was funny to see the steaming bread burst out between her fingers and smear what she called her lousy engagement ring. Out again, on tiptoe, then back, and the birds reconvened. There was one robin, its breast an impudence, too bright, a gash, since everything else, the laurel hedge, the rhododendron bushes, the railing wire, the posts and the numerous trees were bandaged in snow. She was watching, engaged.

'You shouldn't have stuck him for that lunch,' I said.

'Oh yes,' she said; I looked and saw that the *bonhomie* had passed.

'I mean,' I said, trying to gloss it.

'You son of a bitch, you come here to blubber, big mouth, do me a favour, stay away, who's cried on my shoulder, who's the one whose kid I had to play Scrabble with, while you screwed and jounced with a black, Uncle Tom no less, who's been Miss Raw Nerve while the rest of us wipe your arse, you've had it boy, you come here without an invite, so you get out, and that's only for starters...' She threw the glass she had been drinking from and as it fell around my feet, I looked at my toes and wondered how I would get out and if I would meet cross dogs on the way to the village. She went to the dresser, unhooked three of the jugs and smashed them on the tiles. Two little white handles stayed on her fingers like rings.

'You rat. You bloody don't,' she said when I started to dial the operator to get a car hire number. She pulled the receiver from me and mashed it as if it were a bone whose marrow she had to get to. Then all of a sudden she was hitting me, punching, saying son of a bitch, calling on God, calling on all bastards, calling on Buzz. It lasted no more than a minute. She let her hands drop to her sides and said foolishly that she hadn't been sleeping well of late, that a cigarette cough kept her awake. I stayed but it was only for appearance sake. Suddenly we were radically sober, sober and ashamed. I lay on the sofa. At intervals she would appear in the doorway and throw in a blanket or a bunch of cigarettes or matches and say 'Catch'.

She made toast for breakfast and cut it into little segments, like croutons. She was doing everything to make up for it and so was I. But our voices were stilted and our looks veiled. We made no reference to the bruise I had. We were terrified that I might be snowed in, so that when the car hooted we both let out a yell of relief as if in fact a reconciliation had occurred.

'I'll walk you out,' she said, and she linked me, but she did not press upon my arm and we did not say any little recouping thing. She said she would put salt and hew a footpath in case the postman came. That farewell for whatever reason carried with it the nugget of all the others and the waves we exchanged were artifice itself.

As it faws to one, it faws.

Another letter from the lad. Even seeing or saying his name gives me such a thrill, it goes through me like a wash or a ripple. I got a longing then to be on the strands with the big breakers riding over me, ducking down and coming up again for more. I know that the water will be my métier again. In blasted Coose, in yon churchyard.

He says:
Have seen a dance dear Mam-ma! Very different. A file of robed men in the proscenium. Bare stage, no props. Drums and stringed instruments. Black togas and high grey hats, to represent tombstones. A ceremonial kiss and then off with the togas to reveal white robes, not pure white, but off-white, of flannel. They dance, in circles, arms out, eyes never raised, swirl after swirl.

You could hear a pin drop. Only the music and the creak of shoes. Swivel after swivel, yet they never touched, they never collided into one another, every one of them independent of every other and yet together, dancing as one, as a whole. Very soothing and at the same time exciting. I will be home soon.

The dawn like doves to come and still the heart doth burst with need.

Oh mine own land, a lifetime away and still near to me now and for eternity. Is there an eternity – there must be, we have such bodings about it. Is it not it that haunts us at night, it and the bogy man and the freshly dead. Oh land of yew trees and forts and the quicken rods, keep old, wear your old age well, and your stately stoop; the rags that hang about you are like mantles, the mantles of knowledge and wise. Young men will try to procure you, you will be wooed by mediators and mercenaries, do not at the eleventh hour barter yourself, do not sell your old soul.

I went back to Coose for Christmas. I harkened to. It was pitch by the time I got off the bus, but soon I got the feel of the place, the hasp, then the stones, as if the stones hadn't budged or changed place, or the track itself except to get further saturated by waters. There were no cow-pats, no cows, he had finished with farming, was living on his pension. Thin times. It was then I remembered the various herds, and their big soft shits, and the flies on them and their promiscuous feelings and their old dun horns rubbing together, their butting, their bawls, the cowpats crusting and drying, the flies swarming else-where, the unbroken spell of summer evenings. The trees and the mounds became familiar one by one. I had a speech prepared. I was to say, 'I am sorry, I haven't writ-ten, I neglected you, I neglect you.' I was going to say it the minute he opened the door as I stepped into the vestibule, and while I was still wiping my shoes on the mat, or failing one, on the dark red tiles. That is why I went, to show some nature, to make my peace. I practised saying it before I got there at all, in the bus, as I lifted the hasp of the gate, as I walked over the gravel drive, and then, most specifically of all, as I entered the region of grass nearer the house itself. The air was sweet and everything hushed, still. My heart pounded, the very same as if I was taking an exam. I could hear the dogs starting up. They were not really barking, they were rehearsing barking, the way a singer does at a party while somebody else is taking the tasselled runner off the piano. They came towards me snarling, but as soon as they recognized it was me, their enmity turned into fawns and licks and wagging of tails. I could see them well, my eyes having got accustomed to the dark. I spoke to them, I said their names and how well they looked for old dogs. One had a growth on her underbelly, which was big and bulbous, like a ballcock, and funny in its hurtful way. I told the dogs how I had come home for Christmas, and I said that yes, 1 would cook the meat so soft that he could eat it with a spoon, spoon it up, and that I would put holly on the overmantel and rags into the jambs of doors to keep the draughts out and that I would have a secret toddy in the pantry from time to time, to bolster the spirits. I already saw Boss as in a tableau by the fire, deciphering things in the flames, pictures, ogres, animals frontwise and profile, maybe even the dead; Boss scratching his head, digging in, the dandruff falling out, dandruff dispersed about his shoulders (would he be wearing a rug or a shawl, would he have deteriorated that much?) and I saw the too-deep sofa, and the representation of the tabby cats as they tried to turn on the hands of a clock to make it nearer their supper time, and I saw two items of bamboo, and the wise old owl; a whatnot, crammed.

The first thing he said when he opened the door was what an hour of night to come home and what a fright he'd got and how long was I staying. I grudged him the cheek that he so cumbrously kissed. He felt it. He said what was wrong. I said nothing, nothing was wrong. I said life was A1 and ran to the fire like someone who wanted to. A young acacia plant had grafted itself on to the log of wood so that there was a very unfamiliar smell, like a temple, as the essences bubbled. He had cut the trees nearest the house, the ash trees and some ornamental ones. He blamed it on the man with the electric saw, said he wouldn't venture to the woods, said you couldn't get workmen for love or money any longer. I asked how he was. He said a horse had to be shot having slipped on the cobbles and broken a leg. The bridling had started up. I knew that I would be gone by St Stephen's Day, the day of the bachelor wren-bird. I should not have come. I was sullen. He was sullen. I gave him his present, of money; but there was no celebration attached to it, he did not even make a pretence of refusing it as he might have in the past. He said it could go towards a storage heater for the hall. I said halls were a devil altogether to heat. He made the tea. We talked about the crops, other people's crops. The artificial tea roses were still there, thick with dust, it was as if they had been plunged in molten dust and were coated in it rather than in some silver or golden dip. I asked which of the four bedrooms I might sleep in. He said 'Please yourself.' He had got into the habit of talking at the top of his voice. He threw water on the fire to damp it down and said, 'I knew you wouldn't renegue me,' giving me a little biff. In him resided the stance, the stare, the wild umbrage prevalent in all the men that I had loved, unloved, betrayed.

'I came,' I said, but it changed nothing. Same moon, same baulk, same null regret.

In the morning I tore up sacking and put the strips on the rhubarb bed, tucked them around the small shoots to protect them from the frost. Useless. I knew that he would not have stewed rhubarb or a rhubarb pie, ever again. He lived now on shop bread and like me was converted to tinned and instant foods. He proposed a spot of visiting. We cheered ourselves up with that. We decided to visit a cousin who had had a bereavement, and scrounge the tea out of him. His sister Ita had died. It was in that brief truce, what with joking and plotting our outing that he handed me the teacloth, unwrapped, and spreading it out on the hedge I read my alternate characteristics. We even laughed.

The driver of the hackney car was most erratic, drove at a snail's pace on the straight road, then accelerated when he came to corners. I had bought a bottle of wine, port, and little knew that before a month had passed I would be visiting a town house here, the Duke's where it was always decanted. The hips and haws were still on the bushes and it was exceedingly mild. His cousin, Marty, didn't know what to say when we sympathized, didn't know how to reply. We stood in the backyard surveying ourselves in the puddles. 'Ye might as well come in, I suppose,' he said, and we followed him into the kitchen where there was a fishing rod and a tangled line in the middle of the floor. All the footstuffs were on the table beside the lit primus, also the heart of the pike, a little heart, moist, fibulating away. The pike proper was in the frying pan, with white lard dolloped over it. I offered to help. The salt would not come clear of the cellar, so damp was the place. He pointed to a safety pin that was for that purpose. The needling part was bent right back and was coated with salt. I looked at the pike, its narrow eyes, its dainty tongue, teeth pointed as thorns and then covered it with a lid of a saucepan. Anything that fixes my gaze has a habit of coming back, taking me off my guard. I even see upper lips with moustaches affixed to them and ladies with Eton crops. Of course I intervene, I say to them, 'Off, be off, Trash.' Then mercifully I see something lovely, rhubarb or vegetation, some incommensurate blue, that might be sea, or then again might be mountain, blends, all together, all separate, flotillas to the sky. His trenchcoat and his galoshes gave out a smell of rain and rainwater. There was a motto, left by forebears, '*Spe vivemus*'. His sister's grey fur tippet lay on the floor with some pups in it. A litter of six. He said he should have drowned them only that we came and took up the time. I had to search in the wardrobe for the glasses. There was his flannel trousers hanging. It was funny, because it was not folded, the two legs were hanging down, jaunty, must have been his from some sojourn of his at a bijou spot. He was gruffness itself. He said 'I suppose you're coining it, Mary,' and he kept his left hand half fisted. There had been a rash on it, that went amok after we'd arrived. It ran all over his hand like a map, or a dye. I poured the wine into the glasses, said how smart they were, tinted glasses with their long stems. He said they were hers, Ita's. She must have got them when she was engaged to a farmer by whom she was later jilted. I thought uneventful her life, uneventful her death. He dished out the pike. I said did he go to dances at all. He said, 'No no. No diversions.' God bequeath to him wet dreams. We sat with the door open, facing an outside stream, a babbling brook as it's called. The only bit of cheerful sound that there was. The outdoors was like a second kitchen, what with the washtub, his laundry, and a slop bucket hanging from the bough of a tree. There had just been a shower and the air was lustrous. The stream. The sky. The incomplete arc of rainbow. They talked about the prices they got for beef. Boasted but never bothered to listen to one another. He put a sod on the fire but it didn't catch. Nothing, not even a flicker. The sky an avenue of colour. The pups were moaning. I said remember the sugar plums he used to give us in the harvests. Lil used to bribe him with a couple of broiling fowl. He'd skin a flea for a farthing. Still, he likes a bit of a court, had a competition once for lady cyclists and rigged it so that his favourite, a Tilly, won, a great uproar altogether, ladies shrieking, spokes whirring, mudguards getting entangled and he himself unabashedly shouting 'Come on Tilly, come on Tilly.' I expect he has other young girls now who come with baskets in the autumn and with whom he has a bit of guff, a bit of sport, in the orchard.

'Oh there'll be more wars,' he said, and rose, giving us the beck to leave. He threw the skin of the pike to the pups and though they did not move, various pink tongues, thin tongues, reached up to lick. It glittered as it dangled from the fork and twirled in the air. It was like a strip of flypaper to which they adhered. We shook hands but he did not see us out. The driver was beep-beeping and in a rage because he'd been offered no refreshments. Boss and I sat in the back, wrapped up in ourselves, moving farther and farther away until we had slid right up to either window and pressed our faces to it. It said 'Soft margins for two miles'. Fields of brown, hedges brown, buried, the dark steaming up out of the grasses, the odd bit of tallyho as a whelping dog chased the car and was struck with one of the driver's unintelligible, galumptious oaths.

There is no magic, no homecoming, no handshake, no loving cup. Ah my little scallywags, you have separateness thrust upon you.

And still the journey is not without its come hithers, not without challenge, not without incentive. When I come to a crossroad and see the ways ahead, the bushes, the little brown birds, the fortress in the distance, and I ask does it have to be made, and then a terrible fever takes hold of me and I go on unwittingly as if to the sound of bugles, though very often it is to the sound of curs. The very flowers of the field get inside my head and the blossom that hangs from the hedges and I talk to them, to the herds, to the humans, and heady on to the thought of the warm inn and the wheaten bread and maybe an ascension.

I am up now, limbering. I don't think I shall miss my beauty sleep. I am in command of an unusual feeling, a liking for everything, especially the day with a nip in it, jack frost, the winter treetops cogitating, the sky vivid because polluted. I have that nice feeling that one has after a convalescence, the joints are weak and the head inclines to reel but the worst is over, the lurid fever has been passed. Oh Lamb of God. Oh my dark Rosaleen, do not sigh, do not weep. O Connemara, oh sweet mauve forgotten hills.

I went down in all harmlessness to bring in the paper and pick up the various circulars that come, and there it was, an overnight, overseas telegram, addressed to me. It was the very same as if this Armenian quilt reunited with its owner, the goat, had the runs, and the pellets brown and shining came squittering out, numerically before my very eyes. A *fait accompli.* 'We will be home Friday a.m.' The humidity didn't agree with her. Bugger her. She said I might like to telephone Saturday as they will need Friday to sleep in and get reorientated. In other words I am to vamoose. It stands to reason. They don't want to come back into their own house and find me here curled by the fire, or on a sofa, or playing scales on the piano. Finding me here would make it my house. Of course I could squat or throw myself at their feet, I could say I have nowhere to go, I could implore, but the thought of that prostration galls me. Making this my umbilicus, begging for crumbs from their shrivelled store. They won't be seeing me on Saturday, they won't be having any little confabulation with me concerning the inventory, hence the breakages, the dining-room table, the sugar bowl, the ignoble graffiti, and the brandy snifters that so joyously got severed from their stems. Moriarty here I come.

The good is oft interred with the bones ... Example, Flaggler, who is no longer on my social register, and sundry people with whom I meant to make walking expeditions, to whom I promised devotion. Oh shadows of love, inebriations of love, foretastes of love, trickles of love, but never yet the one true love.

'Begone, begone,' everything seems to be saying it, shrieking it, the mirrors, the ingots, the silver cockatoos, and the beautiful brass Portuguese chandelier that I meant to swing out of, but didn't. Even old Instant Humility is in a grump. Begone, begone. Or maybe it's me that's saying it. Already I have such a dislike for the place, such a loathing, an aversion, vengeance for the roof under which all the auspices were tawdry. Oh life's crucible, oh strange latitudes, oh golden birds, heady drinks, poisons, elixirs, let me partake of you yet again. Au revoir Tig, au revoir Jonathan, au revoir Boss and Lil and all soulmates, go fuck yourselves. I have been saddled long enough. It is time for memory to expire.

Gladly, too gladly I go. I refuse to touch my favourite surfaces, or to say anything in the way of a bardic farewell. The harp that once through Tara's halls is silenced, mute. No doubt the time will come when I will think of her with liking, the big pantry, the excitement over visitors, the evenings summoned up by lamps, the spare rooms that I so faithfully aired, the one little room where I sat and heard the impending silence, the tiniest stirs, and lived, though marginally, most sweet, most wholesome hours.

Oh star of the morning, oh slippery path, oh guardian angel of mortals, givvus eyes, lend us a hand, let's kip down on some other shore, let's live a little before the all-embracing dark descends.

Edna O'Brien in Penguins

'Miss O'Brien is an expert on girls and their feelings
... No writer in English is so good at putting the
reader inside the skin of a woman' – *Evening Standard*

The Country Girls

This famous first novel introduces two delightful
heroines, Kate and Baba, and a host of other Irish
characters in unpredictable situations.

Girl With Green Eyes

The comic and poignant sequel to *The Country Girls*
in which Caithleen Brady finds romance in Dublin –
classy romance with the second Mr Gentleman.

Girls in Their Married Bliss

Readers of the previous two novels will not be
surprised at the tragicomedy of the married lives of
Kate and Baba.

Casualties of Peace

Willa had loved and been hurt by love so she tried
to shut out the threat of feeling but the tension in
her world mounts until it is bound to snap.

Edna O'Brien in Penguins

August Is a Wicked Month

Ellen was alone in London, separated from her husband. Bored and frustrated, she decided to go south in search of sun and sex – but found it was not quite as easy as that.

The Love Object

The heroine of each of these short stories swings in her different way between euphoria and agonizing disappointment.

A Pagan Place

In a stream of image, impression, expression, experience and bitter fact of life, Edna O'Brien catalogues the almost delicious agony of the poor Irish child.

Zee & Co

Edna O'Brien explores the sexual geometry of the eternal triangle – and discovers some acute new angles . . .

Mrs Reinhardt and Other Stories

'The stories are . . . varied in setting, in style and in execution . . . they retain the odd, stubborn energy, the baffled resilience that triumphs over humiliation of spirit and circumstance . . . the sensuous perception which brings such pleasure to her readers' – Frank Tuohy in *The Times Literary Supplement*

A CHOICE OF PENGUINS

☐ *Small World* **David Lodge**

A jet-propelled academic romance, sequel to *Changing Places*. 'A new comic débâcle on every page' – *The Times*. 'Here is everything one expects from Lodge but three times as entertaining as anything he has written before' – *Sunday Telegraph*

☐ *The Neverending Story* **Michael Ende**

The international bestseller, now a major film: 'A tale of magical adventure, pursuit and delay, danger, suspense, triumph' – *The Times Literary Supplement*

☐ *The Sword of Honour Trilogy* **Evelyn Waugh**

Containing *Men at Arms, Officers and Gentlemen* and *Unconditional Surrender*, the trilogy described by Cyril Connolly as 'unquestionably the finest novels to have come out of the war'.

☐ *The Honorary Consul* **Graham Greene**

In a provincial Argentinian town, a group of revolutionaries kidnap the wrong man . . . 'The tension never relaxes and one reads hungrily from page to page, dreading the moment it will all end' – Auberon Waugh in the *Evening Standard*

☐ *The First Rumpole Omnibus* **John Mortimer**

Containing *Rumpole of the Bailey*, *The Trials of Rumpole* and *Rumpole's Return*. 'A fruity, foxy masterpiece, defender of our wilting faith in mankind' – *Sunday Times*

☐ *Scandal* **A. N. Wilson**

Sexual peccadillos, treason and blackmail are all ingredients on the boil in A. N. Wilson's new, *cordon noir* comedy. 'Drily witty, deliciously nasty' – *Sunday Telegraph*

A CHOICE OF PENGUINS

☐ *Further Chronicles of Fairacre* 'Miss Read'

Full of humour, warmth and charm, these four novels – *Miss Clare Remembers, Over the Gate, The Fairacre Festival* and *Emily Davis* – make up an unforgettable picture of English village life.

☐ *Callanish* **William Horwood**

From the acclaimed author of *Duncton Wood*, this is the haunting story of Creggan, the captured golden eagle, and his struggle to be free.

☐ *Act of Darkness* **Francis King**

Anglo-India in the 1930s, where a peculiarly vicious murder triggers 'A terrific mystery story . . . a darkly luminous parable about innocence and evil' – *The New York Times*. 'Brilliantly successful' – *Daily Mail*. 'Unputdownable' – *Standard*

☐ *Death in Cyprus* **M. M. Kaye**

Holidaying on Aphrodite's beautiful island, Amanda finds herself caught up in a murder mystery in which no one, not even the attractive painter Steven Howard, is quite what they seem . . .

☐ *Lace* **Shirley Conran**

Lace is, quite simply, a publishing sensation: the story of Judy, Kate, Pagan and Maxine; the bestselling novel that teaches men about women, and women about themselves. 'Riches, bitches, sex and jetsetters' locations – they're all there' – *Sunday Express*